King of the Trenches 3

Lock Down Publications and Ca$h
Presents
King of the Trenches 3
A Novel by *Ghost & Tranay Adams*

King of the Trenches 3

Lock Down Publications
Po Box 944
Stockbridge, Ga 30281

Visit our website @
www.lockdownpublications.com

Lock Down Publications
Like our page on Facebook: Lock Down Publications @
www.facebook.com/lockdownpublications.ldp
Book interior design by: **Shawn Walker**
Edited by: **Jill Alicea**

Stay Connected with Us!

Text **LOCKDOWN** to 22828 to stay up-to-date with new releases, sneak peaks, contests and more…
Thank you.

Submission Guideline.

Submit the first three chapters of your completed manuscript to ldpsubmissions@gmail.com, subject line: Your book's title. The manuscript must be in a .doc file and sent as an attachment. Document should be in Times New Roman, double spaced and in size 12 font. Also, provide your synopsis and full contact information. If sending multiple submissions, they must each be in a separate email.

Have a story but no way to send it electronically? You can still submit to LDP/Ca$h Presents. Send in the first three chapters, written or typed, of your completed manuscript to:

LDP: Submissions Dept
Po Box 944
Stockbridge, Ga 30281

DO NOT send original manuscript. Must be a duplicate.

Provide your synopsis and a cover letter containing your full contact information.

Thanks for considering LDP and Ca$h Presents.

Chapter 1

Toya was sitting on the couch painting her toenails when she heard the front door unlock. She pulled her gun from where it was wedged between the couch's cushions and called out to Ramone. When she upped her gun to shoot the possible intruder, the front door swung open and Ramone stepped inside. A look of relief came across Toya's face and she lowered her gun.

"Bae, you didn't hear me calling your name? I was about to start busting," Toya told him. "I didn't know who it was coming through that door."

"Shorty, who else could it possibly be with a key?" Ramone held up his house key.

"True. But with alla the shit we're involved in, you never know what's gon' pop off. Now gimme a kiss." She threw her arms around his neck and kissed him like a wife would her husband coming home after long hours at the office. "Damn, bae, you smell like weed and alcohol," she said, catching a whiff of his scent. She looked at the two duffle bags in his hands and then at his Timbs. There were dots of dried blood on the toes of both of them.

"I thought you boys were just going to grab a few shots and watch some hoes shake some ass. What's this?" She pointed down at the blood on his boots.

Ramone looked down at the crimson stains on his Trees. "Ma, to answer alla your future questions about shit like this, any time you see me with blood on my shoes, it's from one of two thangs. One, I ran into a nigga I got static with and we banged it out. Two, I was out making moves to net me a bag." He set the duffle bags on the kitchen table. He watched her unzip both of the bags while he removed his jacket and hung it on the back of the chair.

"Damn, how much is this?" Toya inquired.

Ramone took her in his arms. "Like a hunnit and fiddy bands. That's not including that bird of raw in there." Toya, holding five ten-thousand-dollar stacks in each hand, threw her arms around his neck and kissed him again. "You thought about that business we discussed?"

Before Ramone had left the crib, he proposed that they take over her father's drug operation. Toya, on the other hand, wanted to sell the kilos at a wholesale price to this nigga she knew Uptown. Since little mama knew the ins and outs of her father's business, Ramone felt that she should handle the logistics side of things while he played the role of enforcer. He only hoped the workers were on board because it would save them the time of having to assemble a new street team.

"Yeah. And I'm with it." Toya smiled, tucking the blue cheese back inside of the duffle bag.

"Cool. We can use this loot to move the fuck up outta here and get the necessities," Ramone told her. "Yo, ma, I'm tryna squash this shit with yo' boy tonight."

"With who? Maurice?" Ramone nodded. "You mean you letting 'em slide?"

Ramone frowned. "Fuck naw. This beef ain't over 'til his bitch ass is dead. That's on gang."

Toya put her hand on her hip and switched her weight to her other foot. "So what do you propose?"

"You gimme that fool's math so I can set it up for us to meet up and let these guns resolve our issue."

"I hear you, babe, but don't chu think it would be better to catch dude slipping?"

"Nah, ma, it's gotta be done this way. This nigga gotta know that when we clashed, I was the better man. Ya smell me?" Toya nodded. "Good. You got my back?"

"Boy, I got'cho front, back, and both your sides," she assured him.

"That's why you're my ride or die." He stared deep into her eyes and they made out. "Look here, I'ma go take a shower, then I'ma holla at this nigga to see where he's at with it."

"Okay."

"You still got his math, right?"

Toya nodded. "Gimme yo' clothes so I can get rid of 'em."

8

Ramone stripped down naked and handed his pile of clothes to Toya. He kissed her and turned to head for the bathroom. She smacked his ass as he walked past her, admiring his physique.

***

Since all the kingpins' girlfriends, wives, and fiancées had upheld their end of the agreement, Olivia called for the second meeting so they could discuss their next move.

Echo carried out her assignment with the knife and gun Olivia had given her. This was the same knife and same gun Paperchase used to kill Blake and his wife. Having been sidetracked, he had given the murder weapons to Olivia to dispose of for him. Unbeknownst to him, shorty had devised a plan with Echo to get her kingpin of a baby daddy, Devonte, out of the way, since she couldn't bring herself to kill his ass. The plan was for her to frame him for the murders and put him away for a very long time.

Though Echo had agreed to go along with the plan, she found it difficult to go through with it when the time presented itself. It took her thinking back to all the shit that no good, trifling nigga did to her for her to complete the task. She waited until Devonte had fallen asleep, slipped on a pair of latex gloves, and wrapped his hands around the handles of the murder weapons, ensuring his fingerprints were on them.

Echo stashed the knife and gun in places she was going to tell Jake to look when they arrived at their home. Once she'd stashed the weapons in their hiding places, she beat herself black and blue and called 9-1-1. Devonte woke up from them banging on the front door and shouting demands. Echo answered the door looking like she'd been to hell and back, sold the police a bogus story she'd cooked up, and the rest was history.

When Echo pulled up outside of Cruzito's establishment, she noticed that she was the last one to arrive. Blanca was standing outside the entrance of the bar wearing the same attire she had been the first time all the girls had met up. Echo turned off her car, slid on her oversized designer shades, and hopped out of her BMW. She exchanged pleasantries with Bubbles and her chauffeur/bodyguard, Martin. Blanca stopped them at the entrance of the bar. She looked Martin up and down, wondering what the fuck he was doing there.

"This li'l shindig is ladies only, homeboy," Blanca said and then extended her retractable baton in case Martin wanted smoke.

"I know," Bubbles replied, directing her attention towards her. "He has to use the men's room, then he'll be gon' 'bout his business, sis."

Blanca thought things over as she took a close look at Martin. He stood there with a solemn face and his hands at his sides. "A'ight, y'all can come in, but after I frisk his big ass. Assume the position, white boy," she ordered with a sway of her finger.

Martin turned his back to her, sliding his legs apart and out-stretching his arms. Blanca gave him a thorough pat down that produced a big-ass Desert Eagle. She tested its weight, then stuck it in the small of her back. "You'll get this blicky back on your way out," she told him. She then patted the ladies down and allowed them inside behind Martin.

Blanca scanned the area before ducking back inside of Cruzito's, slamming and locking the door behind her. Unfortunately, she didn't spot the Nigerians sitting in the Mercedes-Benz 600 a block away. They had been watching the spot since Olivia and Blanca showed up. The one that had planted the bomb inside of the bar sat in the front passenger seat with the detonator in his hands. He pulled up the antenna of the device, flipped a couple of switches on it, and lifted the see-through covering that covered the red deto-nation button.

Together, the Nigerians counted down, lifting a finger as they did so, "Three, two, one!"

Ka-boom!

The explosion rocked the entire area and set off the alarms of cars parked up and down the block. The Nigerians smiled and bumped fists. The Nigerian in the driver's seat cranked up the Mer-cedes, pulled away from the curb, and drove past Cruzito's bar. The reflection of the establishment shone on the passenger window as the Nigerian riding shotgun looked up at it proudly. He watched as smoke slowly began to rise from the shady business. Having seen enough, he pulled out his burnout cellular and hit up his boss.

***

Sanka, dressed in his red silk pajamas, sat on his throne, stroking a lion cub. An incoming call garnered his attention. Seeing it was the Nigerians he'd sent to handle a very important task for him, he adjusted his Bluetooth and answered the call.

"Hello?" Sanka spoke into the telephone.

"Happy birthday, boss," the Nigerian replied.

"So glad to hear from you, thank you so much." Sanka smiled.

Fuckin' half-breed bitch, that'll teach chu to speak to royalty in such a manor, Sanka thought as he disconnected the call. The smile on his face was replaced with a more serious one. He placed another call for what would be one of the biggest shipments of Rebirth he had acquired in all of his years in the dope game.

Chapter 2

Paperchase was as angry as bees in a hive being swatted by a stick. He'd definitely heard Olivia's conversation with whomever she was talking to and it made him sick to his fucking stomach. Shorty had played him for a fucking chump and to add insult to injury, the bitch planned on bodying him after she was done with him. He was both angry and hurt because he really did love shorty. He saw a future with her that he never saw with any bitch he fucked with.

That's what my black ass get, son. I didn't have no business fucking with big bro's bitch, so I rightfully deserve whatever this hoe got lined up for me, Paperchase thought as he stood before the medicine cabinet mirror brushing his teeth. His gun was laying on the porcelain sink right beside the soap dispenser. *I'm not going out like a sucka though. I'ma give it to shorty and whoever this buster-ass nigga is that's supposed to be her baby daddy. When I catch up with them, they gon' feel a gangsta's pain, real talk.*

Paperchase's cell phone had been ringing nonstop. He checked to see who was calling a few times before he went to the bathroom and every time it was a blocked call, so he didn't answer it. He considered turning it off, but it was his personal number and everyone he had mad love for had it.

"Goddamn, Blood, you a persistent muthafucka!" Paperchase said, agitated, as he picked up his cell phone and answered it. "Fuck's up, Blood? Damn!"

"What's up is you and me linkin' up tonight to settle this beef once and for all," Ramone replied with a dangerous edge to his voice. The young nigga was in full demon mode and ready to wild the fuck out.

"Yo, who the fuck is this?" Paperchase asked, walking aimlessly around his bedroom.

"The nigga that was bustin' at cho hoe ass the other night."

"The white boy?"

"You's a whole bitch, son. You got that many niggas tryna blow yo' shit back?"

"Yo, what the fuck is this shit all about? Why you gotta problem with me?"

Ramone got as hot as fish grease then. "Nigga, don't play fuckin' stupid with me! You know exactly what this shit is about, and it ain't ending until yo' ass lying somewhere stankin', word to Jayshawn."

"Wait. This Ramone?" A confused look crossed Paperchase's face. "Young King, you think I got somethin' to do with what happened to yo' fam?"

"I hear you, my nigga, you's a real fuckin' goofy. But check this fly shit out, bruh. 'Less you wanna spend the rest of yo' life duckin' and dodgin' bullets, I suggest you strap up and meet me alone at this address..." Ramone gave Paperchase the address.

He searched through envelopes and loose papers until he found something to write on. He grabbed an ink pen, snatched the top off with his teeth, and quickly jotted down the location and time.

"The last man standin' wins. Good luck, fuck nigga." Ramone hung up.

Paperchase looked at his cell phone like the nerve of this little nigga before pocketing it.

A'ight, li'l homie. We're on demon time now. You wanna play with the guns? Well, we're gonna play all night long, Paperchase thought while strapping on a white bulletproof vest and slipping a sweatshirt over his head. He made sure both his FNs were fully-loaded and tucked them in his waistband. He slipped on his puffy jacket and pulled his beanie over his head, adjusting it to his liking.

***

Ramone, who was dressed in all black, hung up on Paperchase and set his cell phone on the kitchen table. He picked up a rolled up $100 dollar bill and tooted up the lines of cocaine laid out in front of him. He rubbed the cocaine residue across his gums and made an ugly face. That shit was so potent it had his entire face and mouth numb.

"What that nigga say, boo?" Toya asked from the other side of the table, where she was adjusting the sighting on her M24. She was wearing a black hoodie and black bandana.

"He's with it," Ramone replied, loading bullets into the magazines of his bangers. His eyes were glassy and red-webbed and snot peeked out of his right nostril. The facial hair he'd grown made him look much older than his sixteen years.

"Told you that Dunn hadda ego. There wasn't no way in hell he was gon' turn you down," Toya told him, looking through the scope of her military-issued sniper rifle.

Ramone finished loading up and click-clacking them thangs and tucked them in his waistband. He pulled a black skully over his short dreadlocks and walked over to Toya. She'd just closed the lid on the carrying case of the sniper rifle and picked it up by its handle.

Ramone glanced at his digital timepiece and looked back up at her. "We better roll out now so we can get there early to set up on this fool." Toya nodded understandingly. "Remember, if I come out on the losing end of this thing, you make sure this muthafucka goes down for good. A nigga soul we'll never rest peacefully knowing he's still alive after smokin' my bro."

"I'm not worried about you coming out on the losing end, baby." she said, caressing the side of his face affectionately. "Yo' Glizzies are laced with armor-piercing rounds, so even if this nigga is rockin' a vest, it ain't gon' do no good."

"I know. I'm just sayin', yo, in case shit doesn't go as planned."

"Understood. I love you, Ramone."

"I love you too, shorty. You're the only reason a nigga hasn't joined big bro up there."

They kissed, killed the lights, and left the house to see what fate had in store for them.

***

Paperchase sent a prayer up to the Big Man in the sky, asking for the odds to be in his favor that night. He grabbed his keys and opened the front door. His eyes widened when came face to face with an unexpected visitor.

"Surprise! I'm home, li'l bro!" Scorpion smiled.

***

Toya lay on her stomach in the gallery inside of the warehouse with loose trash obscuring anyone's view of her. She blended in so well within the shadows that she couldn't be seen. In fact, the only person who was aware of her presence was Ramone. He was pacing the ground in front of the Audi truck Jabari had gifted him. He occasionally took a bump of coke from what looked like an aglet to calm his nerves and prepare him for what fate lay ahead. As confident as he was in his gun game, his mother hadn't raised a fool. Paperchase had been an animal in the streets far longer than he had and from what he'd heard, he was raised as a shooter.

After taking a bump of powder, he pulled on his nose and shook his head. The euphoria the narcotic brought him was something else, and he welcomed its effects with open arms. The way Ramone saw it, if tonight was to be his last night on earth, he wanted to be as high as a spaceship when he was knocked off his feet. That way he'd never even known what hit him.

Toya checked the sighting on her military-issued sniper rifle for what felt to her like the one hundredth time in the past twenty minutes. She glanced at the time on her digital timepiece and saw that it was thirty minutes past the agreed upon meeting time they had with Paperchase. Her face was beaded with sweat from the dirty, lint-covered blanket she was under so she wiped it. She then held her wrist up to her mouth so she could communicate with Ramone.

"Babe, you sure this nigga coming?" Toya asked through the radio transceiver.

"I don't know, shorty. I hit this fool up like fifty million times and his bitch ass still hasn't answered," Ramone replied. "I guess homie got cold feet. Maybe alla the gangsta shit I heard he was about while I was a pup was a load of bullshit."

"Nah. It's like I told you before baby, Maurice is a G," Toya said. "His ego is entirely too big for him not to show face. If he hasn't shown up in alla this time, then——" She got quiet, looking out the corner of her eyes, thinking. "Ah, shit!"

Ramone upped his piece, swinging it between entrances of the warehouse. He was anxious and itching to pop any niggas that posed a threat to their lives. "What? What's up? What chu see?" he spoke to her through the radio transceiver in his sleeve as he lowered his gun at his side.

"I just had a thought. If he hasn't shown up yet then maybe he's setting up an ambush," Toya reasoned.

"You're probably right, ma. Hold up." Ramone ran out of both ends of the warehouse to see if he saw anyone lurking or any approaching vehicles that looked suspicious. He didn't see shit, so he ran back inside of the warehouse and tucked his piece inside of his waistband. Cupping his hands around his mouth, he hollered up at Toya. "I'ma hit this nigga one more time. If he doesn't answer, then we're outty."

"Okay, baby," Toya replied. While he busied himself making the call, she looked through her scope for anything suspicious. All she saw was the occasional scurrying rat and flies swarming around.

"Yo, babe, this scary-ass nigga ain't answering. Let's get the fuck outta here!" Ramone shouted up at Toya and waved her down.

She slipped the strap of her M24 over her shoulder and hurried down the metal staircase.

***

Jabari slipped his knapsack over his shoulder and adjusted its strap. He glanced at the time on his cell phone and pocketed it. "Look, I'ma head to the spot and stash this loot. Y'all two fools take shifts overnight watching shorty until I come back in the morning. No fuckin' around with her. Just keep your eyes on her. That's it." He motioned his finger to Jibbs and then Spank. "That goes double for you, nigga."

17

"Fuck you mean that goes double for me, Blood?" Spank frowned, genuinely offended.

"Like I said, nigga, you heard me. The hood talks." Jabari mugged him.

"Oh, so we're believing what these niggas and bitches are gossiping about now? Say it ain't so, big homie. I thought we were better than that." Spank argued.

"Take it however you want to, Slime. It is what it is," Jabari told him. Spank waved him off and finished stashing his cash inside of his bag. "Jibbs, my nigga, lemme holla at chu for a quick second."

Jibbs picked up the crooked branch that doubled as a staff and as a spear. He'd found it inside of the living room among other miscellaneous items that made it apparent someone was living inside of the old house. Grunting, Jibbs used the staff to get up on his feet and limp over to Jabari. Jabari hung his arm around Jibbs' shoulders and walked him toward the back door.

"Look, son, I want chu to keep your eyes on ya boy over there. You know how he gets down."

"No doubt. I'm already knowing." Jibbs said, dapping Jabari up.

Jabari looked over his shoulder at Spank, who was sitting down at the kitchen table. His hand was cupped around the blunt hanging out of his mouth while he was putting fire to the end of it with a lighter. When he spotted Jabari looking at him, he blew a cloud of smoke at him and gave him the evil eye.

"Real shit. Don't let the kid outta ya sight, ya hear?" Jabari told him.

"Most def." Jibbs nodded.

"Good. I'll be back at noon tomorrow."

"A'ight," Jibbs replied.

Jabari patted him on his arm, mugged Spank over his shoulder and walked out of the back door. Jibbs locked the back door behind him and made his way back inside of the kitchen.

"Dunn, what the fuck was that nigga Jabari saying about the kid? And keep that shit a G," Spank said, taking another pull from his blunt. Smoke moved around him animatedly, like it had taken on a life of its own.

"I'ma keep it alla way real wit'chu 'cause you my dawg and I fucks wit'chu hardbody," Jibbs began, tapping his fist against his chest. "Big homie wants me to watch yo' ass 'cause he doesn't trust you around shorty in the basement."

"And why the fuck not?" Spank asked heatedly.

Jibbs stared at Spank like, *Nigga, you can't be serious.* He and Spank knew he had a penchant for violating women. In fact, he garnered the nickname Dopefiend Rapist for luring unsuspecting junkies into his lair with the promise of heroin in exchange for sex.

"I think you know, son," Jibbs told him.

Spank frowned. "And you believe that bullshit, bruh?"

"Shiiiit, you know my motto. 'It's better safe than sorry'," Jibbs replied.

"You's a cold-ass nigga, bro. Straight up." A furious Spank pointed his finger at him before walking away.

Jabari was right to have you watching me. It's just too bad it's not gonna change a fucking thing, 'cause one way or another, I'ma get me a piece of that African ass, even if it means goin' through you to get it, Spank thought as he opened the back door and stepped out into the night's air. A devilish smile spread across his lips as an idea came to mind on how he was going to get Jibbs out of the way so he could have Sankeesy to himself.

Chapter 3

"Bitch, when did you get out?" Paperchase grinned, trying to hide his shocked expression. He didn't expect his brother to show up on his doorstep. Given the circumstances, he didn't know whether to embrace him with a hug or slugs. He decided to try to see where his head was before he made that decision.

"Not long ago," Scorpion replied, opening his arms for a brotherly hug.

Paperchase reluctantly hugged him. He made note of his wearing a bulletproof vest. That meant he was most likely strapped as well.

"You know, baby bruh, I get the feeling you're not too happy to see me."

"Nah, nah, it ain't like that, bro. I just gotta lotta shit on my plate right now," Paperchase assured him. "On top of that, nigga, I didn't expect you to show up today." He threw a playful punch at his shoulder.

Scorpion countered with a couple of playful punches of his own before brushing past him and motioning his coldblooded killas in behind him. They were both wearing hoodies but only one of them was rocking a blue Washington Nationals snapback. The other was wearing a blue bandana tied around his forehead like Tupac Shakur. These Puerto Rican savages represented the crip side of the Woo.

"Right, right, right," Scorpion nodded as he rifled through the refrigerator like he paid rent up in that mothafucka. "Excuse my manners, Slime. My two chaperones, Jay Flocc and Scuddy, y'all li'l niggas meet my li'l bruh, Paperchase."

Paperchase threw his head back like "What's up?" The coldblooded killas mugged him and sized him up. Scorpion turned around, tossing his chaperones small bottles of Simply Orange juice. They caught them and copped a place to sit. One of them opened his bottle and took a drink while the other set his bottle of orange juice on the coffee table. He eye-fucked Paperchase like he was trying to intimidate him. The tension in the air had Paperchase on edge. He still wasn't able to gauge his brother's reasoning for popping up at his crib unannounced, but the vibes he was getting weren't friendly at all. It took all he had to stop from upping his tools and clapping shit up.

Paperchase kept a close watch on Scorpion as he walked back inside of the living room, drinking his bottle of orange juice. He caught a glimpse of the pistol grip shotgun hidden in the recess of his leather duster. He knew from experience that Scorpion usually toted that kind of firepower when he planned on putting in some serious work. Scorpion plopped down on the couch and patted the empty spot beside him for Paperchase to sit.

"I'm good, bruh-bruh. As a matter of fact, I was finna bounce up outta here," Paperchase told him, pointing his thumb over his shoulder at the front door. "I was thinkin' after I make this move, we could hit up Off The Wall for a couple of drinks and catch a tits and ass show."

"Now I know you've gotta few minutes to spare for yo' big bro. Wherever you gotta be, them niggas can wait. And if they can't, fuck them," Scorpion said with a daring look in his eyes. He gave Paperchase the impression that if he didn't do like he said, then he would drop his ass right where he stood.

Paperchase took a breath and walked around the couch. He didn't sit beside Scorpion. He sat on the shorter sofa so he could see everyone inside of the living room.

"So, I'm just curious." Scorpion scratched his temple and locked eyes with Paperchase. "How long have you been fuckin' my bitch?"

The living room became so quiet Paperchase could literally hear a fly soaring around. The fly landed on Scuddy's hand, which was near his waistband. Paperchase swallowed the lump in his throat while holding his brother's gaze. It looked like he was trying to read him as he took another drink from his bottle of orange juice.

"What? What the fuck are you talkin' about, Blood? I'm your brother. I haven't laid a paw on O," Paperchase told him convincingly. "Being locked up has really fucked with yo' head, my nigga." He tapped his finger against his temple.

Scorpion held up a finger for silence, then set his bottle of orange juice down on the coffee table. Paperchase was about to draw his gun and start spitting heat when he saw him reaching inside of his duster, but he fell back when he withdrew a cell phone. Scorpion pulled up something on the cellular and set it on the coffee table in front of Paperchase. He nodded at the cellular for Paperchase to pick it up, and he did. Paperchase went through the pictures, which were of him and Olivia going to different five-star hotels, restaurants, and movie theaters. The last thing that came up was a video recording. Paperchase looked up from the screen to Scorpion, who was eye-balling him hatefully, jaws pulsating. He nodded to the cell phone in Paperchase's hand, signaling for him to play the video. Paperchase tapped the screen and an incredibly loud audio of him fucking Olivia the night he'd broken into her house filled the living room.

"My own flesh and blood; my li'l brother. You lied to my face and you stabbed me in my fuckin' heart!" Scorpion said, clenching his jaws and mock stabbing himself in the heart with an imaginary knife. His nostrils flared and tears fell from his eyes unevenly.

"Bro, I—" Paperchase cut himself short, seeing movement out of the corner of his eye. Scuddy swatted the fly from his hand, but Paperchase had mistaken it for him going for his gun. Swiftly, Paperchase pushed off the floor, upping both his poles and firing back-to-back to back. Scuddy did a little dance as he was lit up like a Christmas Tree on the night of December 25th. He fell to the floor awkwardly, knocking over the chair he was sitting in, in the process.

As soon as the sofa collided with the floor, Paperchase came back up on his knees extending his guns over the sofa.

Bocka, bocka, bocka, bocka!

Jay Flocc took one two to the chest, the side of the neck, left eye, and cheek. He dropped his piece and fell back dramatically. Before he could grace the floor, Paperchase was turning his twins on Scorpion and let them ride!

Bocka, bocka, bocka, bocka!

"Arrrrr!" Scorpion hollered as he rounded the corner inside of the kitchen. He'd just taken one in the back before he disappeared out of Paperchase's sight. Luckily, he'd strapped on body armor before he'd chosen to come holler at Paperchase. Otherwise, he'd be in a real fucked-up situation. He leaned up against the refrigerator, gripping his shotgun with both hands. He looked at the dead faces of his killas and wished they'd opted to wear vests as well.

"This is what'chu wanted, right? This what'chu came here for, huh?" Paperchase asked with his back against the sofa, holding his smoking guns at his shoulders.

"Fuck you, nigga! You betrayed me - your own fuckin' brother!" Scorpion shouted from the kitchen harshly, spit jumping from his lips. Tears danced in his eyes. His brother's backstabbing hurt him to the core of his soul, and now he wanted him to feel how he felt.

"Really, my nigga? All this behind a bitch?" Paperchase shouted over his shoulder.

"Not just any bitch. *My* bitch!" Scorpion roared. He swung out from his hiding place, jacking off his shotgun and firing twice. Sparks flew out of the barrel, puncturing holes through the sofa Paperchase was hidden behind. He turned his face away from the sofa as big holes were torn through it.

"I guess this shit ain't gon' end 'til one of us is dead, huh?" Paperchase shouted out to him.

"It's either that, or you gimme the Rebirth plug," Scorpion replied.

"The muthafucka I'm dealing with wants three bodies in order for us to move forward," Paperchase told him. "Why do you think I haven't been hitting you with any more work lately?"

"Hold up, bitch. You mean the reason why I haven't been getting no product is 'cause yo' gump ass haven't dropped the bodies the connect is askin' for?"

"That's right! For some reason he wants Jabari to be one of those three bodies, but I can't bring myself to drill 'em."

When Scorpion heard him say this, it seemed to make him angrier. He scowled and squared his jaws, gripping his shotgun tighter. "You mean to tell me we're missing out on millions of fuckin' dollars 'cause you don't got the balls to smoke yo' closest homie, yet you we're willing to slide up in my fiancée? Me, your

24

brother, the nigga you share a bloodline with? Bitch, fuck you and everythang you stand for!"

Scorpion swung out from his hiding place, pumping and firing his shotgun back-to-back. Paperchase retreated to the hallway with the doorway exploding around him, drywall and white smoke clouding the air. He ran into his bedroom, flipping on the light switch and throwing open the closet door. He tucked one gun inside of his waistband and kept the other pointed at the doorway. He looked back and forth over his shoulder while rummaging through his closet. By this time, Scorpion was creeping through the living room with his shotgun at the ready. He stepped over one of his killa's dead bodies and kicked the sofa aside. He placed his back against the wall of the doorway and held his shotgun up at his chest.

"What would Pops say if he knew we were going at it like this, huh? Brothers. Tryna drill each other over some pussy," Scorpion heard Paperchase from his bedroom. He didn't know it, but he was chopping it up with him to buy himself time to get what he was looking for.

"Given the circumstances, he'd understand it isn't exactly the woman, but the principle," Scorpion told him, taking shells out of his jacket and loading them into the stomach of his shotgun. "Pops knew his oldest boy was a fuckin' warrior. It's that Nigerian blood coursing through my veins."

"I feel you, big bruh, 'cause I'm a warrior too." Paperchase reminded him, turning around with a grenade and pulling out its ring. He looked up and saw Scorpion's shadow cast on the hallway wall. He ran to the doorway of his bedroom and pitched the grenade forward. It tumbled down the hallway toward Scorpion as he swung out with his shotgun. His eyes bucked upon seeing the grenade bump against his foot. Paperchase slammed his bedroom door shut and dove over his bed.

"Shiiit!" Scorpion cussed, running from the grenade before it could explode. He'd cleared half of the living room before it went off in the background. The force behind the blast sent him flying through the living room's picturesque window. He landed on the front lawn covered in broken glass.

Scorpion, whose face was covered in tiny bloody cuts, pushed up from the ground groaning. He shook the broken glass off him and looked up. His vision was blurry and he was seeing double. When his vision came into focus, he saw Paperchase running across his line of vision with two duffle bags. He threw both duffle bags into the front passenger seat of his ride, turned the key in the ignition, and burned rubber down the street. He was halfway down the block when the residents began to emerge from their homes to see what was going on.

Scorpion used his shotgun to push himself up from the ground. He took off running towards his car, tripping and falling in the process. His flying through the living room window had left him disoriented. He snatched open the door of his whip, tossed his shotgun in the passenger seat, and turned the key in the ignition. He turned out of his parking space and burned rubber down the block just like Paperchase had.

Scorpion stopped at the stop sign at the end of the block looking from left to right. Paperchase's car wasn't anywhere in sight. He didn't know which way to go. Frustrated, he slammed his fist against the steering wheel. "Fuuuuuck!" He slammed his fists against the steering wheel over and over again. Breathing hard, he took out his cellular and sent a group text out to all the niggas that fell under the Woo umbrella.

***

Paperchase blew through stop signs and intersections. He kept an eye on his surroundings and gripped his gun in his lap. He didn't know where his brother would pop up from, but he had to be ready for him. Scorpion was like God to him and many niggas that pledged allegiance to that Woo shit. He molded them all in his image, teaching them the ways of a gangsta. How to move, act, and more importantly, how to drill. Given the fact he'd come up under his tutelage, Scorpion knew what moves he would make before he'd even made them, so his war tactics had to be unorthodox.

Paperchase left his gun lying in his lap and took out his cell phone. His eyes bounced back and forth from the windshield to the screen of his jack as he dialed up Jabari. He focused his attention on the road ahead as he listened to the phone ringing.

Chapter 4

Olivia stood in the back room, greeting all of the kingpins' wives and girlfriends with a smile as they entered through the door and took their seats. Blanca walked around the table laying napkins in front of them. She came around with a platter of hors d'ouvres, allowing them to select a food of their choosing. Next, she presented them with a selection of champagne and let them have their drink of choice. Lastly, she poured up their champagne flutes and slid the bottles back into the buckets of ice.

Olivia smiled excitedly and rubbed her hands together. "Blanca, are we ready to begin?"

"Not just yet," Blanca replied. "Bubbles' boy is in the John. Once he's outta here, it's a go."

"Is she talking about that Zaddy that drove you here the last time?" Lucinda asked, holding the flute in her hand and sitting with her legs crossed.

Before Bubbles could answer, Trinica interjected. "Yeah. That's him. I don't usually do the pink meat, but I'd take Opie for a spin around the block a time or two."

"I know that's right." Lucinda laughed and dapped up Trinica.

Olivia smiled and shook her head. Then she pulled her cell phone out of her purse and took a look at the time. "It's been a while. You sure homeboy isn't in there takin' a shit?"

Bubbles shrugged before taking a sip of her champagne. "Beats the hell outta me."

"Blanca, do me a favor and see what's keeping him."

"Ooooooh." Echo looked over at Blanca and held up a finger for her attention. "Before you do, can you gimme another glass of bubbly?"

"Damn, ma, take it easy. That's like your fourth glass since we've been up in this piece." Trinica told her with a wrinkled brow.

"Sure thang, mama, what would you like?" Blanca asked, turning back around from the door and heading back over to the big bucket of champagne.

"It doesn't matter, love, just fill her up," Echo slurred, holding up her flute.

Trinica locked eyes with Olivia and mouthed, "What the fucks up with this bitch?", throwing her head toward Echo. Olivia waved her off and mouthed, "Leave her alone." She knew Echo was getting faded to cope with the fact that she'd sent her baby daddy to prison for possibly the rest of his life. Blanca knew as well, which is why she didn't raise a fuss about pouring her another glass of champagne after she'd put the alcohol on ice.

Blanca snatched a bottle of whatever out of the ice bucket and made her way over in Echo's direction. She pulled the cork out of the bottle and winded up dropping it to the floor.

"Mierda, estúpido culo botella (shit, stupid-ass bottle)." Blanca scowled as she watched the bottle roll underneath the table, spilling its contents.

***

Martin leaned his head back as he relieved himself at the urinal. He wrapped up his business and washed his hands at the sink. He studied his reflection in the wall-to-wall mirror and was satisfied with the man he saw staring back at him.

Martin was a six-foot, second-generation Russian Jew with a shiny baldhead and a reddish-brown five o'clock shadow. He had broad shoulders and a sixty-inch chest. His overall physique was a true testament to a strict diet and workout regimen. Martin had a military background, a work history in Homeland Security, and ties to the Russian mafia, thanks to his father. After his brief stint in the streets, he decided to make his living the legal way. He took on the duties of an armed bodyguard, offering his services to the wealthy and powerful.

Martin dried his hands and walked out of the men's restroom. He went to go get Blanca so she could lock the door behind him. The back room's door was cracked open, so he could see movement. As soon as he opened the door, he saw Blanca rising from underneath the table with what looked like an explosive.

"What the hell is that?" A frowning Olivia approached from her left, taking a closer look.

"I don't know. It was strapped underneath the table, but it looks like a—"

"BOMB!" Martin hollered, slamming the metal door and diving to the floor.

Ka-booooom!

The bomb exploded with a force as powerful as the wrath of God Almighty. The entire bar was racked! Beer mugs, shot glasses, and champagne flutes clinked together. Some of them dropped off the shelf and shattered on the floor. The beer, champagne, and liquor bottles clinked together, and some of them fell from where they were shelved also. The light fixtures and part of the ceiling fell on the pool table, bar, and the table and chair setup. A white fog clouded the entire establishment. The sound of crackling fire and electricity surging through loose wiring was present.

Martin lay on his stomach, covered in so much debris it looked like he had been rolling around in flour. Groaning, he slowly pulled himself up to his feet. He blinked his eyes and shook the debris from the explosion off him. He picked his nose and wiped it with the back of his fist. He looked around, taking in all the damage that Cruzito's had sustained. Then his eyes stretched wide open, remembering that Bubbles was inside of the back room when the explosion had occurred.

Martin tugged on the metal door repeatedly, trying to open it. He then pounded against it, shouting for Bubbles and them.

"Fuuuck!" Martin shouted, punching and then kicking the door. He pulled off his sports coat and slung it aside. He unbuttoned the sleeves of his shirt and rolled them up to his elbows. He looked around the bar for anything he could find to get the door open. When he couldn't find anything, he dashed over to the bar, searching everything stored behind it. He came up with a crowbar sitting among a box full of wholesale receipts and some other shit.

Martin ran over to the metal door, hearing fire trucks and police car sirens. He discovered the door was raggedy and barely holding onto its hinges, thanks to the explosion. He figured he wouldn't have much trouble getting it open. Martin planted his feet firmly on the floor and stabbed the crowbar into the slight opening of the metal door. He squinted his eyes and clenched his teeth, working the crowbar back and forth. Bwop!

Martin slung the crowbar aside and stepped through the door. He was horrified when he came across the gruesome sight. Most of the women were laid out with one or more body parts missing. They were covered in soot and debris. The entire room was cloudy with fog from the explosion and there were small fires scattered throughout the floor.

Martin looked over the dead faces of all the women, shaking his head and feeling sorry for them. He crossed himself in the sign of the holy crucifix and searched for Bubbles among the bodies. He identified her rather quickly thanks to the tattoo of her man's name on the side of her neck. She was trapped underneath a light fixture. It took some time, but he managed to lift it off of her. He dropped down his knees beside her, panting. He looked her over. Little mama was laid out, staring up at the ceiling. The left side of her face was charred and her eye was a milky white. She was undoubtedly dead, but he couldn't live with that fact.

"No, no, no, noooo!" Martin said over and over again. He hated to think that Bubbles was dead, so he was going to do everything he could to revive her. Taking her by her lower jaw, he blew air into her mouth and performed CPR on her. He repeated this process three times before he finally gave up. Placing his hands on his knees, he closed his eyes and bowed his head. He had a moment of silence for her, closed her eyes, and then he whispered into her ear, "I swear on my honor, I'm gonna find the cocksuckers behind this bombing, Bub. And when I do, they'll pay with their blood. You have my word."

Martin looked alert, hearing someone coughing from somewhere within the room. He couldn't really see shit on the account of the fog being so thick. Holding his arm above his brows, he narrowed his eyes and searched the back room carefully. He came upon Blanca, whose clothing was scorched onto her back. Part of the back of her head was missing and there was shrapnel embedded in her.

Olivia was underneath her and her entire face was covered in debris. It looked like she'd been hit in the face with a handful of baby powder. She coughed and looked around through narrowed eyes. From the looks of it, Blanca had sacrificed her life to save her cousin from the blast.

Martin pulled Blanca's lifeless body off Olivia and took a good look at her. Her face was partially covered in tiny bloody cuts. She had shrapnel stuck in her right eye, the side of her neck, and her left arm was broken.

"Olivia? Olivia, isn't it?" Martin asked, leaning closer so she could hear him.

"Y—yes—" Olivia managed to reply.

"Do you know who was behind this? Huh?"

Olivia nodded. "If they—if they find out I'm alive, then they'll—they'll send someone else to finish the job."

"Who, Olivia? Who? Gimme a name, a place, an address, something for me to find the bastard that did this," Martin pressed her, balling his fists at his side. *Come on, kid, gimme something to work with so I can make these motherfuckers pay. Seventeen years I've been doing this job and I've never lost a client. Ever!*

"It was—it was, uh…" Olivia lost consciousness before she could give him a name.

"Goddamn it!" Martin slammed his fist against the floor. He scooped up Olivia, carried her out of the back room and out of the establishment. "Help! Someone help me." He looked around at the police officers as they hopped out of their cars and approached him. The firefighters were coming up behind them, rushing towards the entrance of Cruzito's.

***

Martin found himself in the waiting room at King's County Hospital going through Olivia's cell phone. He was hoping to find any clues that would single out someone that wanted to see her dead, but so far, he hadn't found any valuable information. Growing frustrated, he deposited the cell phone in his shirt pocket and lay back in the chair. He closed his eyes and said a prayer to God. He asked that He saw Olivia through her surgery so that when she came out, she could finger the bastard that had planted that bomb back at Cruzito's bar. The only thing on his mind was murder and revenge, and he wasn't going to let anything or anyone stand in his way of getting it.

Since New York City didn't give its citizens any permits to carry a concealed firearm, Martin stashed his piece in a safe place inside of the bar. He knew for sure Jake was going to frisk him and ask a shit load of questions, and he didn't want to be caught with his banger. The last thing he wanted was to be way out in the Big Apple fighting a gun charge when he was trying to track down his employer's killers. That would be a pain in the ass that he wasn't up to dealing with. He'd rather focus on the mission at hand.

Martin recalled Olivia saying that whomever was after her was going to send more hittas once they discovered she'd escaped The Hands of Death. Not long ago, he'd watched a news report about the bombing at Cruzito's. Olivia's face appeared on the screen and they put her out there as the lone survivor. Martin cussed under his breath because he knew that whoever the fools were had to be connected to a very powerful man since they went so far as to set an explosive to get rid of her and shit. Since he'd denounced his ties to the Russian mob, he'd have to get at the opposition alone on some one-man army shit. If he was going to do that, then he was going to need some heavy firepower to hold shit down.

With that thought at the forefront of his brain, he called in a favor from one of the few friends he still had in the game.

Chapter 5

Vasili was a very high-ranking member within the organization. He'd taken a liking to Martin and treated him more like a son than his old man. Even after Martin had turned his back on the family, he still kept in touch with him. Martin knew if he hit him up, he wouldn't hesitate to assist him with whatever he needed, which was why he didn't have any gripes with calling him.

An hour later, the old man's cousin Igor pulled into the medical facility's parking lot in a triple black Chrysler 300. Its windows were blacked-out. On top of that, the bitch was bulletproof and bomb proof. Igor showed him all of the hidden compartments where he'd stashed all of the weaponry. He had everything from handguns to assault rifles. The older man even offered his assistance in bearing arms against whoever Martin had smoke with, but he humbly declined. Martin didn't want the old head's death on his conscience if he was to die going to war behind him. He was already putting Vasili's life in danger by associating with him when he was supposed to have washed his hands with him. If higher-ups found out about Vasili still keeping in touch with Martin, they would have him killed along with anyone else who had knowledge of their endeavors.

Igor protested, but Martin wouldn't budge on his decision. So he wished him luck and left the lot in Bubbles' platinum-grey Rolls-Royce Ghost. Martin returned to the waiting room, where he consumed a hot cup of black coffee and played the waiting game while Olivia went under the knife. He began to doze off when the doctor who had performed Olivia's surgery woke him up and gave him an update on her. She'd lost her left eye, had a hairline fracture, a slight concussion, and had a broken arm.

"Well, how is she?" Martin asked.

"She's sedated. Trust me when I say she's going to need a lot of rest," the doctor told him. "If I were you, I'd go home to get myself some rest as well and come back up here tomorrow."

"Yeah. You're right. I've had a long day and could use some shut eye," Martin replied, rubbing the back of his neck and yawning.

He rose to his feet and extended his hand. "Thanks, doc." The doctor shook up with him and left the waiting room.

Martin faked like he was going to the elevator lobby, but as soon as the doctor wasn't looking, he made a detour to Olivia's room. He bypassed a wheelchair and a gurney posted up against the wall inside of the hallway. He looked up and down the corridor to make sure there weren't any eyes on him before ducking inside of her room. He shut the door gently behind him and locked it. Then he crept over to Olivia's bedside. Shorty's left eye and half of her head had been wrapped in bandages and she was wearing a hospital gown. Her left arm was encased in a cast since it had been broken. She appeared to be fast asleep, but Martin would find out soon enough that looks were deceiving, because as soon as he'd gotten close enough, she leaped forward and took a swipe at him with a scalpel.

"Arrrrrrr!" Martin staggered backwards, gritting and grabbing his arm. Blood spilled from between his fingers and dripped on the floor. His forearm felt like it was engulfed in flames. He looked up at Olivia like she lost her goddamn mind. "Grrrr, what the fuck, kid? I come in here to make sure you were good and you fucking take a swipe at me."

"Who the fuck are you?" Olivia asked with a scowl, holding her dripping scalpel out at him. She was a little woozy from the sleep medication they'd given her but she was more than prepared to fight for her life if need be.

"It's me, Martin, Bubbles' bodyguard." Martin clenched his jaws in pain. He rushed over to the sink, where he rinsed his wound with cool water. He then whipped out his handkerchief and wrapped his wound with it. His blood saturated it quickly, but it would have to do until he got somewhere where he could properly take care of it. "I take it you forgot the conversation we had after that explosion."

"That was you? I thought you were Jake or something," Olivia told him, wiping the bloody scalpel off on the bed sheet. She then tucked it inside of her cast in case she'd need it.

"Nah. It was me." He winced.

"I'm sorry. I didn't mean to lash out at you like that, yo." Olivia gave him a sincere apology. "But I thought you were one of his goons coming to knock a bitch off. Ya feel me?"

"It's okay. Given the circumstances I understand where you're coming from." he pulled up a chair and sat down beside her bed. "I need you to tell me who this guy that's after you 'cause I'm going after him for what he did to Bubbles."

"Bubbles? How is she? Matter of fact, how are all of the girls?" Olivia asked with wrinkled brows. Then it was like the explosion back at the bar suddenly hit her and she covered her mouth. She looked at him with a wealth of worry in her eyes. "My little cousin Blanca, what happened to—"

Martin's head dropped. He didn't know how to break the news to her, but his reaction was enough for her to know what was up. She broke down sobbing. Tears dropped from her eyes as her shoulders rocked. He placed a comforting hand on her shoulder and she seemed to rock harder. That's when he pulled her in and embraced her like a loving father would his daughter. He rubbed her back up and down and consoled her as best as he could.

"They're all—they're all dead?" Olivia asked, voice cracking with emotions.

Martin nodded slightly and said, "Yeah, kid. They all died in the blast." He held her at arm's length and looked into her eyes. "Listen to me, this shit is not over. Whoever this motherfucker is, I'm gonna see to it that he pays for his sins, but I'm gonna need your help finding 'em. Okay?"

Olivia nodded with a drenched face and snot bubbles oozing out of her nose. Martin snatched up a handful of Kleenexes from out of the colorful box sitting on the nightstand and handed them to her. He rubbed her back soothingly as he blew her nose and wiped it.

"Listen, kid, if these people are as dangerous as I believe they are, then we've gotta get outta here," Martin told her. "Now, I'm a fierce hand-to-hand combatant, but I'm sure whoever this prick sends isn't coming here for an old-fashioned street brawl."

"You're right. Sanka is a very wealthy man and his resources are limitless," Olivia assured him.

"Sanka, huh? I'm willing to bet my left nut this guy isn't from the land."

Olivia shook her head no, "Uh-uh, he's from Nigeria."

"Okay. We've gotta get chu outta here," Martin replied, peeking behind the curtain of the patient next to her. He found a younger white girl fast asleep. She had short cherry blonde hair and pale skin. Her leg was encased in a cast and her foot was elevated above the bed. Martin slipped over to her closet and took a good look at her clothes. She had a light-gray hoodie with "Boss Chick" across the chest, black skinny-jeans, gray Ugg boots, and a simple black beanie. He could tell just by eying it that Olivia would be able to fit it, so he helped her get dressed in them. While Olivia busied herself putting on the beanie, Martin slipped out of her room and scanned the hallway. The gurney that was up against the wall had vanished, but the wheelchair was still there. He pulled the wheelchair into Olivia's room, helped her into it, and rolled her out. They went right past the hospital staff without them noticing them.

***

Martin pushed Olivia through the automatic double doors of the hospital's exit and was taken aback by what he saw before him. Half a dozen black-on-black Yukon Denalis with Nigerian flags on either side pulled inside of the parking lot. The windows of the vehicles were so black that it was a wonder if any of its passengers could see out of it. As soon as Martin and Olivia saw all of those big body trucks, their stomachs did somersaults. Something told them that those SUVs were carrying some of Sanka's deadliest killas.

"Play it cool, kid, our ride is right over there." Martin nodded to the Chrysler 300 Igor had dropped off to him.

"Which one?" Olivia asked, looking around the parking lot.

"Black Chrysler. It's bulletproof too, so don't worry. Once we're behind those tints, we'll be out of here."

All of the Yukon Denalis parked around or on either side of Martin's Chrysler. The doors of the trucks popped open almost simultaneously, and sure enough, some mean-mugging Nigerians hopped out. They were dressed in all black and wearing Corona-virus masks. They made their way toward Martin and Olivia with the air of an intimidating force. Martin and Olivia's hearts raced and nervousness settled into their minds. Martin couldn't help wishing he had a gun on him or at least a knife, for that matter. He'd studied under his sensei for years and he'd molded him into a lethal weapon. He was confident he could take out at the very least half of the killas before he'd be overwhelmed and killed himself.

"Look, O, these masks may not be enough, so try to avoid eye contact," Martin told Olivia, keeping his eyes glued on the killas. "These guys may know what you look like, but you're wearing that beanie pulled down low enough and half of your face is bandaged. That's a pretty good disguise. These assholes may not even notice ya."

"I got chu," Olivia replied in a low tone. She bowed her head and played asleep.

Martin lowered his head, but kept his eyes on the killas coming his way. His heart beat like an African drum and he clenched the handles of the wheelchair. Gritting his teeth, he prepared himself to engage the overwhelming odds if need be.

"Okay, kid, here goes nothing," Martin said loud enough for only Olivia to hear him.

Sanka's killas walked right past Martin. Some of them looked him right in his face and even glanced down at Olivia but none of them bothered to stop them. Martin sighed with relief once they were clear of the killas. He rolled Olivia towards his Chrysler and glanced over his shoulder at them. They poured in through the double doors of King's County, approaching the front desk.

Olivia jumped out of the wheelchair and hopped into the front passenger seat of the Chrysler. Martin resurrected the vehicle, grabbed a gun from one of the hidden compartments and laid it down on his lap. He then sped out of the parking space in reverse, threw that bitch in drive, and blew out of the parking lot.

Chapter 6

Spank went to McDonald's, which was right around the corner from the house they were holed up in. He got his order and dipped into a nearby CVS pharmacy. He bought a box of Benadryl, popped the lid on Jibbs' cup of Sprite, and dumped as many of the capsules in it as he believed were necessary. Smiling deceptively, he stirred it with a straw and secured the lid on it. He then drove back to the house.

"Goddamn, son, it took you long enough." Jibbs opened up the door and stood aside so he could walk in.

"I could say the same thang for you, long as yo' ass took to open up this fuckin' door," Spank replied, walking inside the house.

Jibbs closed and locked the door behind him. Then he made his way over to the kitchen table by way of the staff.

"Bitch, you went and got some weak-ass Micky D's? Awww, man, I coulda went for anythang but that shit," Jibbs complained while he rummaged through the bag.

"Nigga, you said get whatever, so that's exactly what I got: whatever," Spank argued, pulling his meal out of the bag and popping a fry in his mouth.

"Well, I guess this shit is better than nothing. You at least get my fuckin' Sprite?" Jibbs took a couple of bites out of his cheeseburger.

"Yeah, I got your precious fucking Sprite." Spank begrudgingly smacked the tainted soft drink down in front of Jibbs.

"Thank you," Jibbs replied with a mouthful. Spank threw him the finger. He grinned and took a long drink of his beverage. "Yo, you got shorty somethin' to eat too, right?"

"Yeah. I got her li'l tribal ass somethin' to eat too," Spank said, setting the food and beverage he'd gotten for Sankeesy aside on the table. He then sat down at the table, keeping a watchful eye on Jibbs. He appeared to be chewing slower and slower and drifting off to sleep.

"Say, bruh, what the fuck you put in my drink?" Jibbs asked with slurred speech, looking at his cup. His voice sounded like one of those Chopped & Screwed songs.

"I didn't do shit to yo' drink, yo. You know that Sprite from Mickey D's is mad strong." Spank took a sip from his straw with a sneaky grin on his lips.

"Bullshit! I swear on everythang I love, bro. If you so much as harm a hair on her head, I'ma bust ya brain," he swore as he blinked his eyes and looked around disoriented. "I may be a killa, but I sure as shit ain't no cock-suckin' rapist."

"You ain't gon' do shit but take a nap, nigga."

Jibbs' face balled up with anger and he drew down on him. Spank came right behind him, drawing his tool. They pointed their guns at each other, wondering who was going to be first to pull the trigger. Spank was about to pump Jibbs full of lead when his eyes suddenly closed and he lost his grip on his piece. He staggered from side to side like an old drunk, dropping his banger and then his staff. He lost his balance, stumbling across the floor, tripping over a chair and crashing to the floor. He lay where he was snoring, chest rising up and then down. The nigga was fast asleep!

Spank finished eating his cheeseburger, balled up the wrapper, and took a drink of his beverage to wash it all down. He belched and rose from the table with Sankeesy's bag of food. Spank picked up Jibbs' gun, tucked it inside of his waistband, and proceeded down the steps of the basement with all the freaky shit he was going to do to Sankeesy dancing through his mind.

***

Sankeesy sat bound to the chair with her head bowed. She'd spent the greater part of an hour trying to squirm her way out of her restraints, but her efforts were futile. She was hot, hungry, and had been sitting for so long her ass and legs had gone numb. She didn't have any idea what her kidnappers planned to do with her once they got the weight they'd demanded for her return. Aware of how their leader, Jabari, got down in the streets, she feared he'd have someone put a bullet in her brain once they were paid so she couldn't tell her cousin of his involvement. Although she hoped and prayed this wouldn't be the case, she accepted that more than likely this would be her fate.

Sankeesy looked around the basement for a door or window that would lead to her salvation. The room wasn't lit enough for her to locate any doors, but she could see a little light shining through the old newspaper covering a nearby window. The window was small, but it was just big enough for her to slide into it and wiggle her way out of it to freedom. All she had to do was somehow slip out of the zip-tie, find something to break the window without alerting the kidnappers, and she'd be as free as an uncaged canary.

Sankeesy went back to trying to work her wrists out of the zip-tie. She winced over and over again, rocking from side to side, trying to slip her hands out of the plastic restraints. The ties were sawing into her wrists, creating red rings around them. Sankeesy had worked up quite the sweat during her struggle. Her forehead was peppered with sweat and she was thirsty as hell. Panting, out of breath, she willed the determination she needed to take another crack at trying to get free again. She was about to give it another try when she heard someone coming down the staircase, making them squeak with every step they took.

Sankeesy dropped her head and faked like she'd been asleep the entire time. Spank, who was now wearing a ski mask to hide his identity, switched hands with the McDonald's bag. He snatched up a folding chair with cobwebs and spiders on it. He set it down in front of Sankeesy and removed the items he'd bought for her from the bag.

"I figured you may have been hungry, li'l mama, so I brought you down a li'l something-something to eat," Spank told her, unwrapping her burger and dumping her fries on the wrapper. He pulled the gag down from out of her mouth. "Yo, shorty, you hungry?" She shook her head no. "You probably thank this shit poison or somethin', right? I don't blame you, mama, I wouldn't trust shit comin' from the niggas that kidnapped me either. Lemme show you it's all good though." He took a bite of her cheeseburger, chomped down a few fries, and washed it down with some of her soda. "See there? A nigga perfectly fine. Bite?"

Spank held out the cheeseburger. She nodded and took a bite out of it. He asked if she wanted some fries. She nodded again and he gave her a few fries. He upped the cup of soda in front of her, she nodded, and he allowed her to take a drink. He continued feeding her until she'd eaten everything. Sankeesy belched. The stench made Spank cringe and then grin.

"Damn, li'l mama, you've been holding on to that one, huh?" Spank smiled at her. She nodded her head up and down. He set the soft drink down on the folding chair and a spider crawled up on it. "Well, I figure since I've done you a favor, then you won't mind doing one for me."

Sankeesy looked up at him with furrowed brows, wondering exactly what the fuck she could possible do for him given the circumstances. Spank pulled his and Jibbs' guns from out of his waistband. He set one of them on the folding chair and held onto the other one. Spank unzipped his jeans and unbuckled his belt. His boxer briefs and jeans dropped to a pile on his black Air Force Ones. His thick, vein-riddled dick with its pulsating head leaked a clear gooey substance. Sankeesy's eyes bucked. She leaned back as far away from him as she could, shaking her head from side to side rapidly. The closer he brought his pipe to her, the further she leaned back into her chair. He grabbed hold of her hair and jammed his gun inside of her mouth. It was so far down her throat she gagged. She could literally taste the gun's metal on her taste buds.

"You's an ungrateful-ass bitch! I thought the hoes from third world countries had more respect for their men than these black bitches out here in the west. I guess I was sadly mistaken." He shook his head in disappointment. "Check this out: you gon' either suck this dick, or I'ma pull out my pocket knife and saw yo' fucking tits off. The choice is yours, ma. I'ma have me a ball either way."

Sankeesy stared at him fearlessly while flexing her jaws. The bitch looked like a She-Devil who was ready to devour his soul. It was too bad that old Spank wasn't fazed by her looks. He already knew what she was getting at by flexing her jaws at him, so he fore-warned her.

"I know what'chu thankin', shorty. You're thankin' as soon as I slide this muthafucka inside of yo' mouth, you gon' bite it off, right?" Sankeesy gave him a look that he read as "yes". "That's what I figured. Trip this though, bitch. If you bite my shit, I'ma carve out your eyes and tongue and turn yo' li'l pretty ass into a jack-o'lantern, ya dig?" The devilish smile vanished from Sankeesy's lips and she nodded understandingly. "Good. Now open up! I gotta big surprise for ya."

Spank shoved himself down Sankeesy's throat and she instantly gagged. It wasn't that homie was too long. It was because his nuts were musty and his dick smelled like stale piss. Her eyes watered and she fought back the urge to throw up. Spank threw his head back and closed his eyes, humping into Sankeesy's mouth slowly. He sped up, making her teary-eyed and making slimy ropes of saliva ooze down her chin. He moaned and groaned as he began fucking her mouth recklessly. She grabbed hold of his meaty thighs to try to get him to slow up, but he wasn't having it. Her eyes rolled to the back of her head, and slushing and squishy sounds filled the air.

"Ahhh, fuck—yes, yes—nasty bitch! You nasty, freaky bitch, you!" Spank looked down at her. Her face was scrunched up and she was making loud-ass gagging noises. The changes in her facial expressions made his pipe harder than it was before. That shit was turning him on! He started stroking up and down inside of her mouth, putting his piece as far inside of her mouth as he could. "Ah, yeah, yeah. That's my shit. That's my shit."

Tears flooded Sankeesy's cheeks and her eyes bucked. They looked like they were about to pop out of her head. The veins in her forehead and neck bulged. He was fucking her mouth so hard and fast that it left her little oxygen. He could see she was struggling to breathe and that excited him. He smiled wickedly and continued to thrust her mouth. More and more slimy saliva spilled over her chin and hung low to the floor.

"Ack, ack, ack, gak, gak, ack!" Sankeesy made funny gagging and choking noises. He gave her four more good pumps before he pulled out of her. His dick was shining from spit and dripping with her saliva. He pumped his piece, swelling and shrinking its engorged head.

Sankeesy leaned forward and purged her stomach. A greenish pink goop with food particles in it exploded from her mouth and splashed on the floor. Her heart raced and she panted like a dog that had been running for a mile nonstop. She threw up again and again. Then she was dry heaving and coughing.

Spank approached her, pumping his shit faster. She tried to turn her head away, but he grabbed a fistful of her hair. He placed his foot on the chair and slipped his dick back in her mouth again. He fucked her mouth like it was the pussy between her legs. She gagged, choked, cried, and threw up again. Everything she'd eaten from McDonald's rushed out around his pole and splattered on the floor.

"Ack, ack, ack, gak, gak, ack!" Sankeesy sounded off again from getting face-fucked.

"Ah, yeah, Blood! That shit turn a nigga on! That shit turn a nigga on a lot," Spank swore, grasping her hair firmer and thrusting faster. The sensation surging up and down his tool felt incredible. He licked his lips and looked down at her again. The facial expressions she was making were about to make him nut up, so he pulled out of her. "I want some of that box, shorty. If that mouth is slamming, then I know that pussy is alla that and then some, word is bond!"

"No, no, no more, please!" Sankeesy shook her head from side to side. A mixture of tears and snot dripped from her chin. Seeing her pleading was falling on deaf ears, she hollered out as loud as she could. "Hellll—"

A vicious backhand slap across Sankeesy's face cut her pleas for help short and she spilled her to the floor. She squirmed like a fish out of water on her stomach with her wrists bound behind her back. Spank stalked towards Sankeesy, stroking his piece and kicking the folding chairs out of his path. "Yeah, I love me a li'l feisty bitch. It makes the sex that much greater."

Turning on her side, Sankeesy looked up at Spank, horrified. The reflection of him walking towards her shone in her pupils.

Ghost & Tranay Adams

Chapter 7

Jabari finished counting up the blue cheese he'd made from the licks he and his demons hit that night. He loaded all of the funds into the digital safe. It was so full he had trouble closing it at first, but he finally managed to get it closed.

"I'ma have to get another safe, son. This the second one a nigga done filled up." Jabari thought out loud, shutting the door on his closet's floor and laying the carpet over it to disguise it. He picked up a duffle bag that contained the bricks of Rebirth as well as the other drugs he'd come up on during various licks he'd hit. He planned on taking the narcotics to another location. The last thing he wanted was for Jake to raid his spot and find the drugs and money there. Should that happen, the D.A. would see to it he was buried under the prison.

Jabari switched hands with the duffle bag and took out his cellular. He hit up this hood rat chick he'd been fucking with real tough. Octavia was the mother of all whores, but she loved his dirty draws and he felt like he could trust her. Shorty had been doing all she could to earn her spot in his rotation of bitches, and he planned on using that to his advantage.

"Yo, Octavia, I'm finna slide through there in like an hour or so," Jabari told her, lugging the heavy duffle bag to the front door. "A'ight, ma, I'll see you then."

Jabari hung up the call and his cell phone started ringing again. In fact, he had a hot line that night. He had a total of 36 missed calls. Some of everyone had been hitting him up! The broads he had in rotation, a few of the homies, that nigga Jibbs, and Paperchase. He was busy so he ignored them all and planned to get back with them once he'd finished handling his business.

Jabari had gotten halfway across the living room when he heard someone knocking at his front door like they wore a gun and badge. His antennas went up instantly. He tossed his duffle bag inside of the living room closet, upped his pole, and tip toed towards the front door. The entire time, the knocking at the door continued. Jabari stole a glance through the curtains hanging over the window. He looked relieved when he saw Paperchase on his doorstep. He sighed and tucked his piece at the small of his back, undid the locks and pulled the door open.

"Damn, son, I hit chu mad times. Yo' jack off or something?" Paperchase asked as he entered his home. He had a hostile expression written on his face and he appeared to be irate.

"I've been mad busy, B. I was gon' get right back at chu after I made this move though. Word is bond," Jabari told him after turning around from locking the door behind him. "What up though, Slime? What's goodie, my nigga?" He dapped him up and gave him a thug hug.

This nigga being alive means one of two things. One, he managed to knock the young nigga Ramone's head off, or two, they haven't clashed yet, Jabari thought. *Either way the li'l nigga still hasn't managed to get the job done. Another reason why you don't send a li'l ass boy to do a grown man's job. Fuck!*

"Big bruh's home."

"Word? When they pop the gate for the big homie?"

"I don't know. But the muthafucka knows about that bitch Liv and me."

Jabari lifted a curious eyebrow. "And he didn't blow yo' head off?"

"He tried to," Paperchase replied. He pulled out his gun, set it on the coffee table, and plopped down on the couch. He exhaled and ran his hand down his face. Jabari walked around the shorter sofa and sat down on the arm of it. He folded his arms across his chest and waited for his right-hand man to fill him in.

Paperchase gave him the rundown of his overhearing Olivia's phone call, his accepting the showdown between him and Ramone, and the shootout with Scorpion and his goons. By the time Jabari had finished taking it all in, he appeared to be overwhelmed. Paperchase had a lot on his plate to deal with and he wasn't sure how to tell him how to go about handling it.

Jabari's cell phone chimed with a text message. He told Paperchase to give him a minute while he saw who it was hitting him up. When he looked at the display of his cellular phone, his eyebrows

50

raised. Paperchase saw his reaction and his face creased with curiosity.

"What's up?" Paperchase asked.

Jabari turned the screen of his cell phone his way so he could see what he had been sent. Scorpion had sent out a group text message in a code only those of Woo could decode. He had given the greenlight for his bloodthirsty savages to bring Paperchase to him dead or alive - preferably alive. He was willing to drop a fifty-thousand-dollar bag on whomever brought him back to him in one piece.

Paperchase finished reading the text message and looked at his gun on the coffee table. Jabari picked right up on what he had in mind to do and shook his head. "Really, nigga? We're practically brothers. You think I'd throw you to the dogs like that?"

"My bad, bruh, but a nigga is on edge right now." Paperchase confessed. "I mean, can you blame me though? Niggas want my head out here so it's hard to trust anyone."

Jabari nodded his understanding. "You can trust me. We're family. Look, mad niggas are gonna be gunning after you now that the big homie has sent out that text. I think it's best that you pack yo' shit and skip town. I'ma get in touch with big bruh and try to smooth things over with him so you can come back to the land."

"Blood, I ain't never ran from nothing in my life, so what the fuck do I look like doing it now?"

"You look like the smartest man I know," Jabari replied. "Listen, you gotta know when to fight and when to run. Now you're my nigga, so I'ma have yo' back come hell or high waters but our two guns versus the entire gang… I've gotta keep it one hunnit. We wouldn't stand a chance."

Paperchase nodded as he massaged his chin, thinking things over.

"Look, why don't chu lay low here for the night. No one knows about this spot. I'll purchase you a one-way flight to Milwaukee. I've got fam out there that will take good care of you. You chill out there, fuck with a couple of bitches while I holla at the big homie on your behalf. How's that sound?"

Paperchase thought things over and nodded his head up and down. He looked at Jabari and agreed to the plan he had in mind. He threw his head back, yawning and stretching his arms. He grabbed his gun and stood up.

"Say, bruh, I'ma crash inside of your guest room. I'm tired as fuck," Paperchase told him, giving him a thug hug.

"A'ight, fool. Get chu some rest. I'ma make this move and get chu that plane ticket," Jabari assured him.

"Love, fool."

"Love."

Jabari watched Paperchase until he disappeared inside of his guest bedroom. He shot Scorpion a text, grabbed his duffle bag out of the closet, and headed for the front door.

***

Scorpion was surprised when he'd gotten the text from Jabari letting him know where Paperchase was holed up. He knew how tight him and his little brother were, so he wasn't expecting him to turn him over so easily. Still, he was willing to take his wins where he could get them. He sent two of his most reliable shooters to link up with Jabari so they could gain access to his crib and do what they needed to do. The shooters couldn't wait to complete the task they were given so they could get broken off. As they waited for Jabari to pull up at their location, they thought about everything they would buy with their earnings.

"I think that's son right there," the shooter in the passenger seat said, glancing up at the rearview mirror.

"Yeah. That's him," the shooter behind the wheel confirmed. He glanced in the side view mirror and recognized the face of the driver pulling up.

Jabari busted a U-turn in the middle of the block once he had driven by the shooters. He drove up beside the driver side of their vehicle and dapped up with the driver. He removed a copper key off the ring containing all of his keys and gave it to the shooter behind the wheel.

"Look, by now he should be asleep inside of the guest room at the house," Jabari informed them. "Now he's strapped, but he won't be expecting y'all since I told 'em no one knows where I live. All y'all niggas gotta do is creep up in there and snatch his ass. I'll advise you two niggas to be careful though. Blood's a savage with them pistols."

"Oh yeah? Well, we're savages with ours, too." The shooter behind the wheel flashed his gun at Jabari. "Shit, the only reason why we're taking his bitch ass alive is 'cause we're lookin' to getta check."

"You muthafuckin' right," the shooter sitting in the passenger seat chimed in before licking his Dutch Master closed.

"Yo, what's yo' cut of this 50 G's?" the shooter behind the wheel asked Jabari.

"I don't want anythang, my G. That bag is for y'all to split."

"That's love."

"Nah, fam, that's Woo. I'm out. Gang, gang," Jabari said, touching fists with the driver.

"Gang, gang," the driver and the passenger replied at the same time. With that exchange, the shooter drove away and Jabari drove away in the opposite direction.

Jabari hit up Octavia to let her know he was officially on his way. Once he stashed his drugs at her crib, he had it in mind to bust her down and get a good night's rest. He'd already told Scorpion's shooters beforehand to holler at him once they'd kidnapped Paperchase, so he expected a text from them later on that night. Since he knew Scorpion's get down, he knew he planned on torturing Paperchase until he came up off his heroin plug before he blew his brains out. With Paperchase's death would come the contract on the last two niggas Jabari needed to eliminate to gain access to the Rebirth. The thought of finally becoming the King of the Trenches brought a smile to his face.

Ghost & Tranay Adams

Chapter 8

Bogus and Monty, the two shooters that had hollered at Jabari, swept the perimeter of his house. There was a small light on in the kitchen, so they assumed it was the one the stove provided. That meant Paperchase was most likely asleep. That would make their job so much easier.

"Easy money, ya heard?" Bogus smiled and rubbed his hands together greedily. He pulled his black tranquilizer dart gun from his waistband and cocked it. Monty tapped his arm and motioned for him to follow him. They walked up to Jabari's front door. Monty took out the copper key and listened closely for any movement on the other side of the door. He didn't hear shit!

"Son gotta be asleep in there," Monty said just above a whisper. He slid the key into the slot of the doorknob, turned it, and pushed the door open gently. He removed his tranquilizer gun from his waistband and slowly made his way inside of the house. The street lights shined at him and his accomplice's back. The only sound they could hear was the one of the faulty smoke detector. It beeped on and off annoyingly.

Together, Bogus and Monty tiptoed across the living room into Jabari's bedroom. They found Paperchase asleep on his side with drool pouring out the corner of his mouth. Bogus and Monty smiled wickedly, seeing their charge was at their mercy. As they crept toward him, his eyes suddenly popped open.

"What the fuck?" Paperchase cussed, seeing the two masked men.

When Bogus and Monty saw him reaching underneath his pillow, they knew he was going for his heat. With that in mind, they had to neutralize him quickly. Monty was the first to react. He upped his tranquilizer gun, pulled its trigger, and a dart stuck to Paperchase's left pectoral muscle like a refrigerator magnet. Paperchase didn't show any signs of slowing down, so Bogus fired a dart at him. The dart stuck to his upper chest. His movements slowed, but now he had a firm grasp on his Glizzy. He'd gotten it halfway from underneath his pillow when Bogus upped his real gun. The money was the least of his concerns now. He had to knock Paperchase's head off before he managed to kill one of them, if not both.

A wide-eyed Monty looked back and forth between Bogus and Paperchase. He had to do something fast or he could kiss that 50 Gs goodbye. Paperchase was swinging his gun around to blow Bogus down and Bogus was moving to do the same. Monty tackled Bogus to the floor, causing his gun to discharge up at the ceiling. Paperchase sent two shots at them that didn't come close to hitting them since he was sluggish from the tranquilizer darts. He tried to shake off the dizzy spell from the darts, but he found it difficult. He got off the bed on wobbly legs, knocking over the lamp on the nightstand, and staggered to the foot of the bed.

"Blood, what the fuck you doing?" Bogus asked Monty, scanning the floor for his gun.

"Dawg, you smoke this fool, and we can kiss that bag goodbye," Monty replied, loading another tranquilizer dart inside of his gun. He whispered something to Bogus, who nodded in agreement. Monty then moved around to the other side of the bed military-style on his elbows and knees. Down on the opposite side of the bed, he watched Paperchase make his way over to Bogus. He stood over him and pointed his gun down at him.

"Who sent chu, nigga? Huh?" Paperchase kicked Bogus in his side. "It was Jabari, wasn't it? Wasn't i—" He burped and vomited a little, staining his shirt.

Monty saw Bogus about to clap him, so he made his move as fast as he could. He upped his tranquilizer gun and fired a third dart into Paperchase's back. Wincing, Paperchase turned around to take a shot at Monty, but Bogus tackled him. They flipped over the bed with Monty's gun going high in the air and landing somewhere on the opposite side of the bedroom.

Bogus straddled a barely-conscious Paperchase, gripped him by his lower jaw, and pressed the barrel of his gun into his forehead. Clenching his teeth, he closed his eyes and turned his head so he wouldn't get any blood on his face.

"The money, Bo! Remember the money," Monty reasoned, rubbing his thumb and finger together, symbolizing the Almighty dollar. "25 Gs apiece, my nigga."

Thinking about all of the money he stood to get for the delivery of Paperchase to his big homie, Bogus put the hammer of his pistol back in place and tucked it back inside of his waistband. Monty handed him a dart over his shoulder. He stabbed Paperchase in the side of his neck with the dart and released its sedative into his bloodstream. Paperchase's eyes fluttered like the wings of a dying butterfly before they finally closed and he fell still.

Bogus sat up against the wall sighing with relief and wiping the sweat from his forehead. He glanced over at Paperchase, who was still knocked out and breathing soundlessly. "Blood a tough one, I'll give 'em that."

"Yeah, never thought it would take that many darts to put Slime down," Monty replied, tucking the tranquilizer gun at the small of his back. He tossed Bogus a pair of handcuffs and told him to cuff Paperchase. He took a red bandana from his right back pocket and dumped the pillow out of the pillowcase that was lying on the bed. Once Bogus had turned Paperchase on his stomach and cuffed his wrists behind his back. Monty gagged him with the red bandana and slipped the black pillowcase over his head.

"A'ight, my nig, let's go get paid." Monty shook up with Bogus.

Bogus hoisted Paperchase over his shoulder and carried him towards the front door. Monty followed closely behind them.

***

Sanka was hot as chicken grease when he found out through the news that Olivia survived the explosion at Cruzito's bar. For as long as he had his killas carrying out missions for him they'd never botched them, so he was willing to give them another chance. Only this time he wasn't sending them alone to carry out the job. Nah, fuck that! The Nigerian drug lord sent scores of his killas to guarantee Olivia's black ass was deceased once and for all.

Sanka called in a favor to have a gun stashed inside of the men's restroom on the same floor Olivia was on. An armed security guard that just so happened to be a light-skinned Nigerian retrieved an extra piece he had back at home on his lunch break. The firearm was what underworld figures called a Ghost Gun and it was virtually untraceable. When the security guard returned from his lunch break, he stashed the pistol and a pair of latex gloves inside one of the panels inside of the men's restroom. On his way back to his post, he texted his contact to let them know where he'd hidden the weapon. Right after, his cell phone chimed with a text message informing him of a $5,000 dollar deposit. He smiled when he saw it, sat down behind the desk at his post, and scrolled through his Instagram.

The Nigerians walked right past Martin and Olivia and through the double doors of Kings County Hospital. The leader of the pack gave the nurse at the front desk a bogus name to look up while one of the other killas slipped away from the group. He gave the light-skinned Nigerian security guard a knowing nod as he passed him, letting him know he was connected to the nigga that had dropped that $5,000 dollar bag on him for the gun. The light-skinned Nigerian security guard returned the gesture and the killa continued past him.

***

The killa got off the elevator on the twelfth floor, wandering down the hallway, looking for the men's restroom. He crept inside of the restroom, locked the door behind him, and traveled down the row of stalls until he found the one he had in mind. He opened the door of the last stall, stepped upon the toilet, and lifted the panel above it. He felt around inside until he came across the latex gloves. He pulled them on and flexed his fingers inside of them. Next, he took the gun down, chambered a round in it, and made his way out of the men's restroom. As he approached a pair of doctors coming his way, he pulled his baseball cap low over his brows and looked down. He glanced over his shoulder to see if they were paying any

58

attention to him and they weren't. The killa looked inside of his wrist where he'd written the number of Olivia's room and the bed she was supposedly in. Once he had it memorized, he spat on his wrist and rubbed the information until it disappeared.

The killa ducked inside of Olivia's room and grabbed the pillow off a nearby bed. He walked over to a sleeping Olivia, placed the pillow over her face, and pressed his gun in behind it. He squeezed the trigger three times and removed the smoking pillow. It had charred holes in it on one side while it was stained with blood on the other. Suddenly, the lights inside of the room popped on. The killa frowned, seeing it wasn't Olivia he'd rocked to sleep but the young white girl who happened to be her roommate.

"Freeze, motherfucker!" a voice ranged from the opposite side of the room.

The killa whipped around and upped his gun to find two pink-faced sheriffs with their pistols pinned on him. They unloaded a barrage of bullets on him and a pained expression spread across his face. The first couple of shots from the killa went wild and completely missed their targets. But that didn't stop him from sending a couple more life-threatening bullets their way before he was eventually chopped down. He stumbled backwards fast, banging the back of his head against the heater and slumping awkwardly against it.

***

"I'm sorry but there's no one by that name that's been admitted here," the nurse told the Nigerian that appeared to be the leader of the pack. He nodded understandingly and apologized for inconveniencing her. "It's okay. Have a nice night."

"You do the same," the Nigerian replied before turning around and making his way out of the hospital.

The rest of the killas fell in line behind him, marching across the parking lot. Everyone had gotten inside of their trucks except for the lead Nigerian. He'd opened the passenger door when he heard mad gunshots coming from above one of the hospital floors.

Fuck, man, the Nigerian thought, hopping into the front passenger seat and slamming the door closed. He pulled his cell phone from the inside pocket of his black leather coat and scrolled his contacts for the killa he'd sicced on Olivia.

"What's up, Abdullah?" the Nigerian driver asked with a scrunched face.

"You didn't hear all that gunfire, Hakim?" Abdullah replied.

"Shit! Akeem is probably in trouble." Hakim went to hop out of the truck but Abdullah grabbed his arm.

"Don't bother. I'm calling him now. If he doesn't answer, then this hit is botched and we're getting the hell out of here," Abdullah assured him before focusing his attention back on the ringing cell phone.

***

The sheriffs cautiously moved in on a bloody Akeem with their guns pinned on him. The entire time they could hear his cell phone ringing over and over again. The ringing stopped and then it started right back up again. One of the sheriffs switched hands with his gun and checked for a pulse in his neck. He looked back at the other sheriff and shook his head no. Akeem was dead. The sheriff that had checked Akeem's pulse holstered his piece, kneeled down to the murder suspect, and removed his cell phone from his pocket. The display read *Abdullah*, but it was spelled backwards. He passed the cellular over his shoulder to the other sheriff. He took it and answered the call.

"Hello? Hello?" the sheriff spoke into the jack. The caller hung up on him.

***

Abdullah ended the call he'd made to Akeem and pocketed his burnout cell phone. Feeling Hakim's eyes on him, he looked at him and shook his head. He knew then that Akeem was one dead mothafucka.

"Shit!" Hakim slammed his fist against the steering wheel. He turned the key in the ignition and the truck came back to life. He swung out of the parking space and sped out of the parking lot.

Chapter 9

Martin took Olivia back to his place, where they had a couple of drinks to calm their nerves. He broke out a yellow First Aid kit and Olivia cleansed his wound and stitched it up. She poured herself another drink and went to sit down on the living room couch. She caught a glimpse of herself in the mirror on the wall and walked over to it. She took a good look at herself, touching her bandaged eye and then the burnt areas of her face. She felt a little depressed knowing she'd never be as beautiful as she once was. It was a hard pill to swallow, but it was what it was.

Fuck it. It is what it is, Olivia thought, shrugging her shoulders.

"Aye, O, why don't chu sit down over here and tell me about this Sanka character," Martin said, patting the empty space beside him.

Olivia plopped down on the couch beside Martin and tucked her legs underneath her Indian style. She swirled the ice cubes around in her glass and then took a sip. "Where'd you like for me to start?"

"The beginning. I needa know what I'm dealing with, honey." Martin took a sip of his drink and rested his glass on his thigh.

Olivia took a deep breath and went on to tell Martin how she'd met Sanka. She winded up bumping into him while she was shopping in a Gucci department store. He was dripping so hard the nigga should have brought his own personal mop with him. She thought he was handsome and found his accent incredibly sexy. They exchanged numbers and promised to link up that night for dinner. They wound up at Mr. Chow's, where they enjoyed their meals over an expensive bottle of wine. One thing led to another and they ended up having sex in the back of his Porsche truck. The next thing she knew, she felt a pinch in the side of her neck and everything went black.

Olivia's eyes fluttered open and she sat up where she was lying. Rubbing her eyes, she looked around, wondering where she was and who had brought her there. She touched her neck where she'd been pinched before she lost consciousness, but she didn't feel anything there. She assumed she'd been injected with some sort of sedative.

When she heard footsteps coming toward her, she instantly looked around for her purse where she'd hidden her pole.

Fuck me! Whoever snatched me up must have taken my shit, Olivia thought. Hearing the footsteps coming closer, followed by a low growling, she looked up ahead. Two lions emerged from the shadows, licking their mouths and eying her hungrily. Terrified, Olivia' eyes bucked and she started crawling backwards on her hands and her high heel pumps.

"Yo, what the fuck? Where the fuck am I?" Olivia looked around wearing a panicked look on her face. She kicked off her shoes and scrambled to her bare feet. She looked around for an escape route.

"Relax, Sleeping Beauty. They will not harm you unless I tell them to, isn't that right, Chibunna?" A commanding voice spoke from somewhere deep within the palace. A moment later, the shadows stirred and Sanka strolled out. The clothes he had on in the Gucci store made him look like a typical street nigga, but now that he was in traditional African garb, he had the appearance and swagger of royalty. Homie had an aura of power surrounding him that intimidated most and made them feel like peasants.

Sanka kneeled to the lion on his right, running his hands through his wild hair and kissing him. The beast placed its huge paws on his shoulders and licked his face. Sanka turned his head, chuckling and smiling. He motioned the other lion over and greeted him in the same manner. He rose to his sandaled feet, ruffling the big cats' heads before advancing in Olivia's direction.

Sanka clapped his hands and two of the Black Barbie Dolls appeared holding his throne. They placed it behind him and he sat down, crossing his legs. One of them gave him his jeweled chalice while the other fanned him with a huge feather. Sanka pulled the cork out of his chalice and took a healthy drink from it. One of the Black Barbie Dolls produced a gold handkerchief and dabbed the wetness from around his mouth.

Olivia got up on her feet, dusting her clothes off. The lions had her feeling queasy, but she tried her best to ignore them while addressing Sanka. "Sanka, what is…what is the meaning behind all of this?"

Sanka gave Olivia the same spiel he had Jabari, Paperchase, and others before them. He even gave her the idea of incorporating a round table of female bosses that could get their weight from him at a very generous price. She wouldn't have to pitch in on the work they'd get if she agreed to have his baby, but if she didn't, she had to come up with her cover charge.

Sanka brought up the fact he was getting up in age and didn't have a male successor to reign over his empire. He'd done his homework on her and knew everything about her, including her Puerto Rican father and Nigerian mother. He felt that with her background, she would be the perfect woman to carry his seed to term. It was very important to him that he had a son soon so he could start grooming him for his birthright.

"Well, what if the kid turns out to be a girl?" Olivia asked curiously.

"Then I'd take care of you. You'd never have to worry about money for the rest of your life," Sanka assured her as he took a drink from his chalice again.

Olivia weighed her options. The way she saw it she was in a win, win situation so she decided to agree with the deal. Olivia nodded her head before delivering her answer. "A'ight. I'm with it, yo."

"Excellent." A smile spread across Sanka's lips. He switched hands with the chalice and extended his hand. "But a deal is not a deal until we shake on it."

Olivia, wary of the lions, hesitantly walked over to Sanka and took his hand. Keeping his eyes on her, he shook her hand gently, then placed a tender kiss upon it.

"Are you hungry, Ms. Suarez?"

"I most definitely am."

Olivia went on to tell Martin about the heated argument she had with Sanka back at Paperchase's crib. She knew without doubt Sanka was the one who planted the explosive in an attempt to kill her.

Martin downed the last of the alcohol in his glass and set it down on the coffee table. He unbuttoned the collar of his shirt, loosened his tie, and turned around to Olivia. "Do you know where this Sanka is?"

Olivia swallowed the alcohol she'd just drunk. "No. That night we ate again and drank. The next thing I knew, a bitch was waking up in the back of an Uber. I figure he must have spiked my drink or something."

Martin massaged his chin as he took some time to think. Olivia continued to drink as she observed the gears turning inside of his head. He took a deep breath and went on saying what was on his mind. "No matter how I look at this thing, we're gonna have to go at it alone."

"You mean you and me?" Olivia motioned a finger between them.   "Yeah."

"Wait a minute, Dunn. I thought you said yo' people with the mob."

"They are but a bounty has been put on my head since I turned my back on the family."

"Fuuuuck, yo! I thought we at least had a little army to back us," Olivia said angrily, sitting her glass down on the coffee table.

"Nope. Sorry, kid, it's just you and I. Now bring your pretty ass on." Martin rose from the couch and pulled Olivia up to her feet.

"Where are we going?" a wrinkled-brow Olivia asked.

"Kitchen. I'm gonna get us prepared for the firefight that's sure to come, and you're gonna make me dinner."

"Oh, I just love a man that takes charge." She downed the last of her drink and set the glass on the coffee table. Martin followed behind her, watching her booty swing from left to right. He feasted his eyes on her assets as he rubbed his chin. She disappeared around the corner inside the kitchen.

Boy, would I love to get behind that. Sheesh, Martin thought before hurrying inside the kitchen behind her.

**

"Helllllp! Somebody helllllp me!" Sankeesy screamed so loud the veins on her forehead looked like they would explode. Spank straddled Sankeesy's waist and laid his gun down beside him. She struggled to get away from him as he held her down and ripped her panties from her. He threw them aside and feasted his eyes on her exposed buttocks. Her butt was meaty and showed faint traces of stretch marks. Little mama didn't have any surgical enhancements. She was all natural and he loved that shit!

Spank smacked her butt cheeks, leaving red hand impressions behind. Sankeesy jerked and squealed from the stinging sensation. Jerking from left to right, she screamed over and over again for help.

"Bitch, didn't I tell you to shut the fuck up?" Spank punched her in the temple and knocked her out cold. She lay with the side of her face on the floor and her eyes rolled to their whites. "This mask hot as fuck, Blood." Spank peeled the ski mask up off his face like it was a layer of skin and flung it aside. He spat in his hand three times and used his saliva as a lubricant. He placed his dick at her entrance and slammed it home. Her walls sucked at him and her heat made him shudder. "Oh, yeah, this shit is gon' be good." He sucked on his thumb and stuck it inside of her crinkle. He gripped a handful of her hair with his other hand and started fucking her. His face balled up and he flexed his jaws. He pumped into her from behind, watching her buttocks jiggle. "Ahhh, fuck, son, I'ma bouta nut up in this pussy!" His mouth stayed stuck open and he attacked her womb savagely.

Sankeesy moaned as she slowly began to regain consciousness. Her eyes fluttered. She could hear Spank's grunting and feel his tool stretching her pussy-hole wider and wider. Her eyes popped open and she started screaming again. He continued to violate her, ignoring her pleas for help. Her entire body jumped up and down against the pavement as he pummeled her sex box.

"Get—get the fuck—off of me! Helllp!" Sankeesy cried, jerking from left to right, trying to get away from the sick, twisted fuck.

Spank went as hard as he could on her, chasing after his nut. At the last minute, he pulled out of her and pumped his meat. Globs upon globs of his hot gooey babies leaped out of his pee-hole and splattered between the crack of her ass. He wiped the sweat from his forehead with the back of his hand and rubbed his dick against the slimy mess plastered on her buttocks. He breathed heavily with his chest rising and falling. Sankeesy cried and whimpered under him. Hearing her infuriated him. He balled both of his fists and started raining blows to the back of her head.

"Shut up, shut up, shut up, shut cho ass up!" Spank drilled the back of her skull mercilessly.

"Nigga, I told you I'm not with that raping females shit!" an angered voice boomed from behind Spank.

He went to grab his gun from off the floor and something heavy crashed into the back of his skull. Splinters flew across the basement and he fell to the floor on his back, wincing. He looked up to see Jibbs standing over him with the now-broken staff. Swiftly, he snatched up his piece and extended to take a shot at him.

Bocka!

Chapter 10

The gun fired as Jibbs swatted it out of Spank's hand with what was left of the staff. The gun slid across the floor and bumped up against the wall. Spank pushed up off the ground to get to his feet but before he could, Jibbs kicked him in his forehead. His forehead split open and oozed with blood. He fell back against the floor, looking up at Jibbs in a daze. Jibbs planted his foot on his chest, grunted, and drove the overgrown stake through Spank's heart. His head dropped against the floor and he took his final breath. Blood poured out of the massive wound in his chest and quickly formed a pool around him.

Still holding onto the staff, Jibbs dropped down to his knees and bowed his head. He breathed hard and sweat slid down his face. He swallowed spit and looked up at Sankeesy. She was crying while Spank's semen dried on her ass. Using the staff, Jibbs pulled himself back up and limped over to her. He lowered himself to the ground, running his fingers through her hair and apologizing to her over and over again.

"I'm so, so sorry, ma. I swear on my life this was not how this was supposed to go down." Jibbs assured her with glassy eyes. "That nigga Spank is a monster. Raping and beatin' on women is not my M.O. Yeah, I steal and I kill, but I don't get down like that."

Sankeesy looked up at him with snot bubbling out of her nose and tears bursting out of her eyes. Her tears obscured her vision, making everything look as if she was looking at it through a crystal ball. When her vision came into focus, she could see Jibbs' face clearly.

Jibbs made note of how Sankeesy was staring at him. That's when he touched his bare face and remembered he'd left his ski mask on the kitchen table upstairs. He couldn't allow her to live knowing his identity. He had to take her out of the game ASAP. Jibbs recovered both guns, aimed them at the back of Sankeesy's head, and looked away so blood wouldn't get into his eyes. Clenching his jaws, he tried to will himself to blow her head off.

Do it, Jibbs, do it. You've peeled mad niggas' caps back before. This should be easy. Jibbs tried to gas himself up to do what he felt needed to be done. He found it overwhelmingly hard to twist shorty being that she reminded him so much of his sister. Her begging him not to kill her was fucking with his head also. She'd sound like herself then other times she'd sound like his sister Josie.

Jibbs was only eleven years old when he watched his sister's crack-dealing boyfriend kick the living shit out of her for not having his dinner prepared when he'd gotten home. He tried to defend her, but he wasn't any match for the brute strength of a grown-ass man. The psychotic fuck pistol whipped Jibbs' so badly that he was left with severe nerve damage that left him with his lazy eye. Josie ended up stabbing her boyfriend in a major artery that resulted in his death. She wound up getting fifteen-years-to-life in the state penitentiary and Jibbs ended up the ward of the streets.

"I can't, I can't do it, yo. I just can't," Jibbs lowered his pistols. He looked at the floor with his chest heaving up and down, wondering what he should do next.

Sankeesy turned over on her side, looking over her shoulder at him. "Please, please, don't kill me. I don't wanna—I don't wanna die, please."

Jibbs tucked both guns at the small of his back, grabbed her under her arm, and pulled her up. He set up one of the chairs and then sat her down in it. When he looked into her face, she reminded him so much of Josie. He badly wanted to comfort her and make her feel better.

"Please, please, just lemme go. I promise, I promise I won't say a word to my cousin about any of this. I swear, I swear on my life," Sankeesy whined then broke down weeping again with her shoulders shuddering.

Jibbs became glassy-eyed and wrapped her in his arms. He shushed her and assured her that everything was going to be okay. "I got'chu, li'l mama, don't worry. Don't you worry 'bout a thang," Jibbs said, whipping a red bandana from his right back pocket. He wiped her wet cheeks and made her blow her nose into his bandana. She winced as he dabbed the blood seeping from her split lip.

70

"Please—you don't—you don't understand. I've heard stories about Jabari. He's a killer," Sankeesy tried to reason with him. "After my cousin gives him what he wants, I'm one hundred percent certain he'll put a bullet in my head and leave me stinkin' somewhere."

"I got'chu, ma. No one's gonna hurt chu ever again. That's my word," Jibbs told her with confidence.

Sankeesy broke down again making an ugly face. "Oh, no, no, you don't understand! You don't under—"

Jibbs grabbed her face with both hands and looked into her eyes. "Listen to me, baby girl, listen." she calmed herself and swallowed a lump of fear. "You're right about that, Jabari is a killer. Spank was too." He kept his eyes on her, but threw his head towards Spank's dead body. "And so am I. But I promise you this, once we get this drop from yo' fam, you're gonna walk away from all of this. You've got my word. You hear me? You've. Got. My. Word."

Jibbs didn't know it, but that nigga Jabari had every intention of putting little mama to sleep once he got that shipment of Rebirth from Sanka. He couldn't risk the blowback he'd get if the Nigerian was to find out it was him that had robbed his spots and kidnapped his cousin.

"How long have you known Jabari?" Sankeesy asked him.

"Since before I could piss straight. I owe the homie a lot," Jibbs replied. "He's the one that took me off the streets and gave me the game so I could eat."

Sankeesy nodded understandingly. "He's done that for you and you're willing to turn your gun on 'em for me?"

Jibbs looked down at the floor for a moment, thinking things over. He looked back up at Sankeesy with a reassuring eye and nodded confidently. "Yeah. As crazy as it sounds, I'm willing to bang it out with the homie behind you." He caressed her cheek with the back of his hand, meaning everything he'd told her. Jabari ranked above him within their organization, so his loyalty was to him. Siding with Sankeesy over him was a clear sign of disloyalty and betrayal. He understood this. But there was something within his heart that told him he was doing the right thing by being willing to go to war behind her.

Sankeesy stared into Jibbs' eyes. They could see themselves in each other's pupils. She touched his face like it wasn't real. Jibbs was about to say something when she abruptly snatched the guns from the small of his back. She pointed both guns into his face. He gasped and threw up his hands, surrendering. He swallowed the spit in his mouth and locked eyes with her. He thought for sure she was going to knock his head off so he braced for the inevitable.

Images of Spank savagely raping her assaulted Sankeesy's mind. Throwing her head back, she screamed so loudly her uvula shook and a vein in her neck bulged. She ran over to Spank's corpse and dumped on it mercilessly.

"I hate chu! I hate chu! I hate chu!" Sankeesy shouted, spit flying everywhere. She shot up her rapist's body, then blasted off his dick and balls.

Her sorrowful cries and the pistols firing rang out in the basement. Still holding the bangers, she dropped to her knees in the pool of blood that had formed around Spank. The blood saturated her dress. Buckets of tears poured down her face and her shoulders shook. She dropped her head and whimpered uncontrollably. Still holding his hands up, Jibbs cautiously approached Sankeesy. He'd gotten within three feet of her when she whipped around and pointed her Glizzies at him. Freezing in his tracks, Jibbs leaned his head back and lifted his hands higher. He didn't know where Sankeesy's head was then, but he was sure after being violated she had it in her to blow him down. She had the look of a killer in her eyes and he'd seen it more times than he cared to count.

"Easy there, shorty, easy," Jibbs said in a calm, soothing voice. Slowly, he reached for the bangers in Sankeesy's hands, hoping she wouldn't change her mind and try to wet him up. Jibbs gently grasped the pistols, and Sankeesy allowed him to take them from her hands. After checking the clips of them, he tucked the guns into the small of his back. He extended his hand toward Sankeesy. Wiping away her tears with a curled finger, she looked at his hand and then up at him. He gave her a reassuring nod. She hesitantly grasped his hand and he pulled her up into him. He was taken off guard when she fell into him and wrapped her arms around his neck. She buried her face into his chest and sobbed. He frowned with his hands up. He wasn't sure what to do, but he figured it was best that he comforted her.

"Shhhhhh. There, there now. I got'chu, mama," Jibbs assured her. He hugged her into him and rubbed her back affectionately. "No one will ever, ever hurt chu again. That's my word, shorty."

Sankeesy calmed down as best as she could and looked up at him. She sniffled as he wiped away her tears. "You—you promise?"

Jibbs nodded. "That's on everythang I love."

Sankeesy attacked him like a wild bobcat, grabbing his face and kissing hungrily. They breathed heavily as they made out. Jibbs walked her backwards as they continued to lock lips. Sankeesy took a step backwards and bumped into Spank's body. She and Jibbs looked down at the bloody mess they'd made of the goon. When Sankeesy looked back at Jibbs, he had a weird look on his face like he'd been placed under a spell.

Sankeesy lifted up his chin so they'd be at eye-level. "What's the matter?"

All of the work he and Jabari had put in together over the years plagued his brain. He'd seen him claim more souls than he cared to recall. On top of that, he wasn't one to leave loose ends, so he'd definitely leave Sankeesy stinking once he'd collected those birds.

Jibbs looked at Sankeesy and the promise he'd made her earlier crossed his mind. "Listen, we've gotta get the fuck up from outta here," Jibbs told her. "I know that nigga Jabari. As soon as that drop is secured, he's gonna—"

"Kill me?" Sankeesy finished his sentence.

Jibbs was silent for a minute before nodding to her question. He could see the terrified look in her eyes. It made him want to love her, hold her, protect her. "Look at me, ma. Ain't shit gon' happen to you that ain't gon' happen to me first. You believe me?"

"Y—yes. I believe you," Sankeesy nodded, blinking back tears.

"Good," Jibbs replied, pulling out both poles and reloading them. He tucked one in the small of his back again and gave the other to her. "Look, it's best we burn this bitch down to rid this place of any of our fingerprints and split with that loot upstairs. As far as Jabari…well, I'll take care of 'em."

Sankeesy kissed and hugged Jibbs again. He held her in his arms and looked up at the ceiling. Jabari had taught him everything he knew about the murder game, so he knew how he'd move in the heat of battle. It wasn't going to be easy to take him out, so he'd have to be on his shit if he was going to come out on top.

"Jibbs, your heart's beating fast. What's wrong?" Sankeesy looked up at him with worried eyes.

Jibbs took a deep breath and swept her hair out of her face. "Nothing. I saw some old-ass lawn mowers on the side of the garage. Maybe there's some gasoline still in 'em. We could use it to douse this place and get outta here," he told her, looking around the basement at all of the items that were sure to go up in flames. "Come on." He grabbed her hand and retreated up the staircase.

Chapter 11

"He agreed to have someone pick that up tonight, so y'all make sure everything is good," Sanka told one of his most trusted men as he stacked gold bars like they were pieces to a Jenga game. "Awright. As soon as that's handled, report back to me as soon as possible."

Earlier, Sanka hit up the dude that had kidnapped Sankeesy and demanded two thousand bricks to get her back. He let him know his drop would be coming tonight. The dude promised Sanka he'd get his cousin back as soon as he made sure every bird was accounted for. He wrote down the address where the weight was being held for pick up. Then he hung up so he could arrange for one of his men to pick up the ransom.

After he'd gotten off the jack with the dude that snatched Sankeesy, Sanka took a Skype call with some very prominent figures - men and women with political and underworld ties that allowed them to get virtually anyone touched, or even killed, for that matter. It was because of these very same men and women that Sanka was able to move his drugs throughout the United States without much interference. People like Sanka and his associates who had millions upon millions of dollars often got bored. This was on the account that they'd seen everything and had done everything. Sanka came up with the idea of pitting three money-hungry demons against each other for a chance to control the heroin trade in Brooklyn, New York. He wanted these people to be connected in one way or another, to see just how far they were willing to go to obtain financial freedom.

Sanka handpicked Paperchase, Jabari, and Olivia to be the three participants in the game. He knew all he needed to know about their backgrounds and felt they were the perfect picks for his challenge. Sanka's associates thought so as well, so they agreed to a friendly wager. They all picked who they believed would succeed in carrying out the executions he'd ordered. Everyone put their money on who they thought would walk away victorious. The betting pool reached just over one billion dollars. Though Paperchase, Jabari, and Olivia were getting dangerously close to killing each other, they'd yet to complete the task they were assigned.

Sanka had grown frustrated with how slowly things were moving so he changed the game up a little. He added new participants to the mix for a fight to the death. The winner would be elected to move his heroin. His father before him, King Uche, had used this method to select his personal bodyguards, wanting only the best of the best watching over him. This was who Sanka had gotten the idea from.

After hanging up with one of his most trusted men, Sanka reached for one of the gold bars when a portrait on his desktop caught his attention. In the picture, it was him at nine years old, his mother, Tangela, who'd unfortunately died from colon cancer two years later, and his father, King Uche. He was the head of the very drug empire Sanka ran today until he was assassinated. The murder of his old man weighed heavily on his mind. Since his passing, he'd had to deal with depression, sadness, and emotional turmoil.

Sanka picked up the portrait of his family and sat back in his chair. He always wanted to be in the position of power he was in today, but he didn't want it to come at the cost of his father. If he could, he'd give up his seat at the head of the table to have his pops there with him.

Sanka's eyes turned glassy and he said, "Long live the king."

***

Jabari had gotten off the jack with Sanka about thirty minutes ago. To his surprise, he already had the weight he wanted in exchange for his cousin's safe return. Though he was happy upon learning the news, he was left with the task of putting together a team to not only pick up the drop, but unload it to be dropped off at the traps he had in mind. He'd hit up Jibbs and that nigga Spank, but neither of them answered, so he got in touch with his other slimes to be at the warehouse to receive the shipment. Among the lot was the homie, Dooda, who had a trucker's license. He was one of the few homies that had a legit gig. On top of that, his gun game was exceptional, which was why Jabari nominated him to pick up the product and deliver it to the warehouse. Dooda wanted fifty bands for his services. Jabari agreed to the requested amount. The way he saw it, fifty stacks was a drop in a bucket compared to the loot he stood to make moving the dope he'd come up on.

Jabari didn't have to bother knocking on Octavia's door. She'd given him an extra set of keys to her crib since he usually stashed shit at her place anyway. Jabari let himself into the house, closing and locking the door behind him. The house was warm and the smell of food resided in the air. He placed his duffle bag inside the living room closet and locked it with his key. The aroma of pork chops, corn, broccoli, rice and buttermilk biscuits led him into the kitchen. He found Octavia cooking and nodding her head to whatever she was playing in her Air-Pods. She was so tied up in what she was doing and listening to that she hadn't heard him enter her home.

Jabari crept towards the twenty-three-year-old BBW, taking in her appearance. Octavia was 5'7" with hazel-green eyes. She weighed a total of 235 pounds and at least 30 of that was attributed to her ass. Her skin was a dark caramel. Her dreadlocks were braided into plaits and hung halfway down her back.

"As much as you run the streets," Octavia began without turning around, startling Jabari. He froze in step. "I figured you'd be hungry, so I whipped you up a li'l somethin'-somethin'."

Jabari frowned. "How'd you know th—"

"Boy, please, I stay on point," Octavia told him. Right then, a red dot appeared on his head and he looked to where it was shining from. Octavia was pointing a gun with an infrared laser from under her right arm. She was so slick with it that Jabari hadn't even noticed she had it pinned on him the entire time.

Jabari smiled proudly and clapped his hands. She was as green as a head of lettuce when he started fucking with her, but she learned how to handle herself thanks to his tutelage.

Octavia turned the fire from underneath the food and removed her Air-Pods. Placing her banger on the counter, she went about the task of preparing Jabari a plate. He helped himself to a glass of Minute Maid fruit punch. Walking past her, he took a drink and smacked her on that big old ass of hers. Loving that freaky shit, she moaned and bit down on her bottom lip.

"You better stop it 'fore you get somethin' started," Octavia said, placing his plate down in front of him. She sat on his lap and picked up a chicken wing to feed him.

"That's what I'm hoping," Jabari said, smacking her on her big, juicy thigh and squeezing it. She smiled delightedly and let him take a bite of the wing.

Jabari finished eating and Octavia wiped his mouth and kissed him. They stared into each other's eyes lustfully while he rubbed that big, bodacious booty of hers. Octavia had some fire-ass pussy and it had been a while since Jabari had put the pipe to her. He told himself tonight was the night he and her box got reacquainted.

"You still hungry?" Octavia asked, rubbing her hand up and down his chest.

"Yeah, I'd like some dessert."

"What'chu want for dessert, pa?"

"Pussy." Jabari grabbed her by the neck, kissing her hungrily.

They jumped to their feet, steadily making out and feeling each other up. He pulled away for a second, smacking everything from off the tabletop and onto the floor. He snatched her big ass up and laid her down on the table. Quickly, he unbuckled his jeans and pulled his boxer briefs down around his thighs. He then assisted her in removing her boy-shorts. Her kitty looked like a moose knuckle. On top of that, it was glistening wet and drooling.

Licking two of his digits, Jabari slipped them inside of her treasure and fingered her vigorously. Her eyes fluttered. She threw her head back and her mouth hung open. She slipped her hands underneath her cut off tank top and stimulated the pierced nipples of her small breasts. Feeling an orgasm rolling down her coochie, her sensual moans grew louder and louder. Jabari shoved his vein riddled penis down her throat and started humping into her slopping mouth. She massaged his nut sack as she sucked him off, gagging and slurping.

"Mmmmm-hmmmmm." Octavia jerked her head up and down Jabari's meat. Her warm, bubbly saliva flowed out of her mouth and poured over her chin. She made funny faces and humped into Jabari's hand as he penetrated her womanhood. A tingling sensation built up in her twat. Her vagina's lips plumped and her secretions ran out of her love hole. Jacking Jabari off, she whined and looked between her legs like she was attempting to push out a baby. Jabari stared at her face as he continued to work her middle. It brought him great pride seeing the pleasure in her eyes. She was reacting like she was possessed and he was eating that shit up. Octavia's legs were wide open and her white polished toes curled. Her clit was throbbing madly and sticking up like a hitchhiker's thumb.

"Ooooou! Oooooou! Oooooooou!" Octavia screamed loud enough to shatter all of the glass objects inside of her house. She shook fast and hard, drenching the tabletop in her natural juices. Jabari rubbed his shiny hand across her clitoris rapidly. The sensation made her rise from off the tabletop on her feet. Shorty looked like an alien spacecraft was trying to draw her up into it.

"Ooooooh, myyyyy Goddddd, Jabarriiiiiii!" Octavia screamed louder this time. She orgasmed so hard her essence flooded the table and dripped off its edge. Going limp on the table, she closed her eyes, moaning and steadily jerking Jabari's pipe.

The look on her face coupled with her moaning had him ready to burst. Using one hand, he grabbed a fistful of her dreadlocks and took his dick away from her with the other. Turning her face toward him, he pumped his meat as fast as he could. She rubbed her face up and down his stalk. She licked it occasionally, enjoying its warmth. When little mama began sucking on his nut sack, he groaned and pumped even faster. The sound of him pumping his meat filled the air.

"Uhhhh, uhhhh, uhhhhh! I'ma 'bout to bust all on yo' fuckin' face, bitch!" Jabari said with a raspy voice, eyes narrowed into slits. He howled like a lone wolf at a full-moon and plastered her face with his hot babies. She moved her face around making sure every last drop hit it. Sweat sliding down his face, Jabari breathed heavily, slipping half of his dick inside of her mouth. He swept her dreadlocks out of her face and listened to her suck his piece passionately.

Chapter 12

"I want some of this pussy. This muthafucka wet," Jabari claimed, rubbing on her pussy. It was warm to his touch. He slithered between her thighs and rammed himself inside of her down to his nut sack. She gasped loudly and her mouth trembled. He placed a leg on each of his shoulders, placed his fists on either side of her, and started long-stroking that pussy. He gave her long, hard strokes, making sure to hit the bottom of that thang. "Yeah. That's what I'm talking about, ma! This my shit! This my muthafuckin' pussy!"

Jabari went in on her, pounding her out. She sank her French-tipped nails into his biceps as he pumped her furiously. She was screaming so loud and he was hitting her so hard the table began screeching across the floor.

"Ahhh, ahhh, shit! Mmmmm! Mmmmm!"

Jabari closed his eyes and clenched his jaws. The pussy was sloppy, wet, and hot as a furnace door. He felt a tingling sensation below his dickhead and he knew he was going to cum any second. He licked around his mouth and laid into her harder. She was screaming loud enough for the neighbors to call the police and report a woman was being killed next door. Still, Jabari didn't give a fuck! He kept on going until he splashed deep inside of her. His buttocks clenched as he flinched three times, releasing all of his seeds inside of her. Jabari, sweaty and sticky, collapsed on top of Octavia, panting. Using her tank top, she wiped her face clean and stroked the side of his head. She stared up at the ceiling smiling and thinking what life would truly be like if she was his girl or maybe even his wife. She held her fingers in front of her eyes and imagined a big-ass six-karat diamond engagement ring on one of them. A vision of her and him standing hand and hand at the altar flashed across her mind.

Octavia kissed the top of Jabari's head and continued to stroke the side of his head. Having finally caught his breath, he looked up at her with beads of sweat sliding down his face.

"You ready for round two?" Jabari asked, grinning. "Mmm-hmmmm." Octavia smiled, wrapping her arms around his neck and kissing him.

Jabari hopped off the table and helped Octavia down. He led her inside of her bedroom, where he fucked her until he was shooting air. They then laid up smoking weed and watching reruns of *Martin*. Octavia, with her head lying against his chest, ran her hand up and down his abs. There was hysterical laughter throughout the night until Jabari's cell phone rang. At that moment, things took a turn for the worse.

***

Martin sat at the kitchen table cleaning his Franchi SPAS-12 semi-automatic shotgun. There were pistols, ammunition, grenades and two black bulletproof-vests on the table. While he was focused on cleaning and loading the weaponry, Olivia was standing over the stove cooking his favorite Italian dish. Occasionally, he'd steal a glance at her shapely body and she'd pretend like she didn't catch him looking. Olivia didn't really dig white men. She had a thing for brothers and Latinos, but she couldn't front on old Martin. He had that masculine, handsome, physically fit, older man look thing going for him. She definitely saw him as a sneaky link in the future.

"Mmmmmm. This sauce in life." A grinning Olivia claimed. She'd just tasted the pasta she'd made from scratch. "You've gotta taste this, Martin." She walked toward him with the wooden spoon, holding her hand below it in case she spilled any of it.

Martin loaded the last shell into his semi-automatic shotgun and laid it on the tabletop. He opened his mouth and received Olivia's pasta sauce. A smile stretched across his face when he tasted it. He nodded and held up his thumb.

"You gotta li'l sauce at the corner of your mouth there, sweetie." Olivia pointed at the corner of his lips. Martin tried to wipe it away, but he wasn't getting it. "Oh, here, let me." She scooped the sauce up from the corner of his mouth and sucked it off of her finger. Lust danced in her eyes as she stared into Martin's beautiful baby blue eyes. They moved in for a kiss, but Martin stopped halfway. His forehead wrinkled on the account that he'd spotted something out of the window above the kitchen sink. Frowning, Olivia popped her eyes back open, wondering why he hadn't kissed her. She looked over her shoulder and a red dot appeared on her forehead.

"Get down!" Martin tackled her to the floor as a sniper's bullet burst through the window's glass. Almost immediately, the lights inside of the house went out. Hunched down, Martin moved to the kitchen table, where he strapped on his bulletproof vest and snatched up his semi-automatic shotgun. He slid the other bulletproof vest to Olivia and she strapped it on. Olivia didn't have a clue that the night Sanka kidnapped her; he downloaded a GPS app to her cell phone so he'd always know her location. That's how his men were able to track her down to Martin's crib.

By the time she'd finished strapping on the body armor, a rush of bullets came through the house, sending broken glass and splinters flying everywhere.

"Goddamn, these niggas ain't playin'!" Olivia said, narrowing her good eye so nothing would get in it.

"No they're fucking not! Here." Martin passed her a semi-automatic pistol that he'd taken from the kitchen table. It was already loaded, cocked, and ready to shoot. "You know how to work one of these?"

The front door rattled as someone tried to kick it down. When that didn't work, whoever was on the other side of the door, sprayed bullets through the door and the windows of the house.

"Get your ass inside the pantry and stay there!" Martin ordered, pointing in the direction of the pantry.

Olivia nodded and obliged his command.

The ruined front door swung open and splinters flew everywhere. Masked African gunmen poured inside of the house with assault rifles. They moved towards the kitchen, spitting carnage and death at Martin. Martin snatched a grenade off the table and kicked that bitch over. It hit the floor hard, spilling all of the guns and ammo. Taking cover behind the kitchen table, Martin stole a peek from the side of it and saw the gunmen moving strategically to take him out for good.

"How the fuck did they know where to find us?" Martin asked no one in particular. He pulled the ring out of the grenade and tossed it over the toppled table. He heard the Africans talking to each other in their native language. He figured they were discussing their next move, but he wasn't sure. He couldn't understand a word of that shit they were speaking.

"It's a grenade!" one of the Africans hollered.

"Runnnnn!" another African shouted.

By then. it was already too late, the grenade exploded, sending Africans flying in every direction. Small fires were scattered throughout the living room and the smoke was so thick. no one could see through it.

Racking his semi-automatic shotgun, Martin stood upright and surveyed his surroundings. He was about to enter the living room to make sure the blast from the grenade had taken out all the African hitters when Olivia called out to him.

"Martin, are you okay?" Olivia called out from the pantry.

"I'm peachy, O. You just stay where you—" Martin was cut short when a bullet slammed into the back of his body armor and made him stumble forward. Cradling his shotgun, he whipped around to return fire and another bullet slammed into the front of his bulletproof-vest. He stumbled back before losing his footing and falling up against the wall. His face balled up as he bit down on his bottom lip to combat the pain. He was as sore as a bitch, but was thankful his vest was reinforced with three layers of Kevlar. Otherwise, his white ass would be on that big basketball court in the sky, hooping with Jesus.

Rapid gunfire chewed through the wooden back door. Then there was the sound of a hunk of metal hitting the floor. Martin assumed whomever it was had shot out the lock of the door so they wouldn't have any problems entering the house.

The back door swung open and the lone sniper walked inside. He was gripping his Knight's SR-25 rifle and looking for those he'd been sent to apprehend. By this time, the smoke detector was blaring and smoke was billowing from the pot of pasta sauce. The smoke was thickening fast, making it hard for the shooter to see. Martin decided to take advantage of the situation. Wincing, he slowly stood up right and upped his shotgun. He pulled it back to back to back, making the shooter drop his SR-25 rifle and spin around. He fell against the kitchen sink and slid down. Before his knees could grace the linoleum, he used the sink to pull himself back up and snatched a meat cleaver from the countertop. Whipping around, he ran at Martin and lifted the blade above his head.

"Aaahhhhh!" the shooter screamed as he ran at Martin, prepared to chop his head off his shoulders.

Martin attempted to pull the trigger of his shotgun, but it locked up on him. Turning it sideways, he took a closer look at it and it was jammed. Grunting, he tried to fix it, but it wouldn't budge. When he glanced up at the shooter, he was on top of him and in mid swing.

Boc!

The shooter's head jerked to the right. He fell to the floor and the meat cleaver clinked to the surface beside him. Blood poured out of the side of his head and quickly formed a puddle. Olivia lowered her smoking pistol at her side and turned the fire off from under the burning pot of pasta. She walked over to Martin and inspected his body to make sure he was okay.

"I thought I told you to stay your ass in the pan—" Martin's eyes bucked seeing a tranquilizer dart stick to the side of Olivia's neck. Her eyes snapped open in shock and she yanked the dart out of her neck. She looked in the direction the dart had come from and lifted her banger to lay down who'd shot her. Before Olivia could put a bullet in her assailant, the contents of the dart took effect and she passed out where she stood.

Martin turned around to find another one of the masked Africans. He went to open fire on him, but forgot he'd never unjammed his shotgun. Looking up from his weapon, he locked eyes with the masked man and his tranquilizer gun. He held the shotgun like it was a baseball bat and ran to knock his head off. The masked man stepped back from his reach and popped his ass twice. The

Ghost & Tranay Adams

tranquilizer darts stuck to Martin's chest like Gorilla Glue. His eyes rolled to the back of his head and he slammed into the kitchen floor.

Having dispatched both his targets, the masked gunman stuck his tranquilizer gun inside of its holster and prepared his victims for transportation.

86

Chapter 13

Buuuuuuuunk, buuuuuuunk, buuuuuuunk!!!

The driver of the semi-truck sounded off the horn while idling at the shuttered door of the warehouse. He glanced at his watch and then he radioed someone who was inside the warehouse. "Open the goddamn shutter, nigga. We don't have all day," the driver said into his walkie talkie before setting it aside.

A moment later, the shutter was coming up fast. There was a hitter on either side of the entrance pulling lengths of chain, drawing the shutter higher and higher off the ground. Once the shutter was all the way up, the semi-truck was driven inside of the warehouse. The hitters that had lifted the shutter lowered it and made sure it was secure. Cradling their assault rifles, the hitters made their way over to the semi-truck. The driver swung open the door of the truck, climbed down to the end of the ladder and jumped down. He made his way around to the back of the semi, taking in the armed hitters walking the catwalk on either side of the tenement. He gazed over his surroundings and there were about ten more hitters on the ground. That was including the ones that had drawn open the shutter.

The driver unlocked the back of the trailer and lifted its shutter. Stacked from floor to ceiling were boxes labeled Folgers. A kilo of Rebirth was hidden inside of each coffee canister. The driver extended its ramp to the ground so they could unload the cargo. He rolled a dolly towards the ramp, but stopped at the end of it.

"Fuck y'all waiting for? Grab some of them dollies so we can start unloading this sh——"

The driver was cut off by the Folger boxes flying out the back of the trailer. He dropped his dolly, ducked, pulled out his pistol, and ran for cover.

The hitters on the ground looked up at the trailer. Their eyes bugged and their mouths flung open. They couldn't believe the force that was coming at them. Nigerian hitters wearing see-through oxygen masks and holding assault rifles spilled out of the back of the semi-truck, catching Jabari's hitters off guard. Before they could react, they were getting chopped down. They screamed as hot bullets burst through their warm flesh and they fell to their bloody demise. The Nigerians charged down the ramp, leading out the back of the semi-truck. They moved around the warehouse, strategically trading gunfire with the niggas on the catwalk and eliminating them along the way.

"Aaaaaaah!"

"Gaaaaaah!"

"Arrrrr!"

Jabari's men hollered, flipping over the guardrail of the catwalk and plummeting to their deaths. The others were cut down where they stood defending themselves. They lost hold of their assault rifles and fell to the catwalk theatrically. The smell of gunsmoke, blood, and the dead's last bowel movements lingered in the air. The Nigerians walked the grounds, pumping rounds into those of Jabari's men who were still alive and moaning painfully.

"Uuuuuuh!" The last among Jabari's hitters moaned as he crawled away from what were his final moments on earth. One of the Nigerians didn't even look his way as he walked by, extinguishing his life with a short burst of gunfire.

The Nigerians started talking in their native language among each other once their job was done. Something within earshot caught the top dog of the African hit squad's attention. He told them to keep talking, but lower their voices in their language. They obliged him. The top dog pulled the oxygen mask off his nose and mouth and removed his ski mask. He slung the ski mask aside, cradled his assault rifle, and hunched down. He moved with the grace of a panther closing in on its first meal of the day. He listened closely to where the voice was coming from. He could hear whomever it was clearly. They were talking as low as they could to someone either on a cell phone or in person. Right then, he knew it was one of Jabari's hitters who had managed to escape Sanka's wrath. But he was going to see to it that he didn't live long enough to tell the tale.

The African hit-squad's leader crept around a cluster of drums to find the lone survivor, who was the driver of the semi-truck. He was hunched down holding a gun in one hand and his cell phone in the other. When all of the gunfire started, he laid down a couple of Africans before taking cover to figure out his next move.

"Nigga, I don't know exactly how many of them mu'fuckas there were," the driver told Jabari. "Once those bullets started flying, I got the fuck outta do—"

The driver's words died in his mouth when he saw the leader of the hit squad. He raised his gun to take a shot at him, but by then, it was entirely too late. A burst of gunfire ripped into his lower intestines and he hollered in agony. Making an ugly face, he fell to the ground, holding his wound. Seeing the leader moving in on him to finish the job, he looked around for his pole to defend himself.

"Dooda? Dooda? Dooda!" Jabari's voice rang from the other end.

Abdullah's shadow eclipsed Dooda as he palmed his pistol. He brought it around to fire, but his eyes bugged once they met the lethal end of an assault rifle. A burst of rapid gunfire blew his wig clean off his head.

"Dooda? Dooda? Dooda?" Jabari continued to call out.

Abdullah picked up Dooda's cell phone as the rest of his hitters gathered behind him. He wasn't even surprised when he saw Jabari's name on the display. He shook his head, thinking of how Jabari fucked up by crossing someone as powerful as Sanka. He pressed the cellular to his ear as he turned around to his men.

Upon learning who was behind Sankeesy's ransom, Abdullah scowled, making himself look like a furious lion. "Jabari, I knew snakes slithered, but I didn't know they could talk."

***

How the fuck did these fools find out I was the one behind the lick? Goddamn, I know this nigga Sanka is about to be out for blood now, Jabari thought. *Fuck it! If I die then I die, just gimme a gangsta's death.*

"Yeah, it's me you antelope chasin' muthafuckas!" Jabari spat heatedly, taking his time to toot cocaine up his nose. He knew it was about to be war time and he wanted to be coked up out of his mind should he go out in a blaze of glory. "You tell Sanka's ol' bitch ass he better come with it, 'cause once the god gets started, I'm not letting up. That's on everythang I love." He reached underneath his pillow for his pistol, but it wasn't there. He felt around for it but he still didn't feel it. Frowning, he turned around to lift the pillow and got the surprise of his life. Octavia was pointing a gun in his face, and she looked like she meant business.

"Bitch, what the fuck is this?" Jabari scowled.

"It's called a gun, Einstein," Octavia replied.

Jabari sized her up. He didn't think she had it in her to rock his ass to sleep. "Shorty, you ain't got the heart to take my life, you love me too much."

"Not as much as I love money, nigga," Octavia swore, cocking the hammer back of her Glizzy. "Now gimme the jack 'fore I blow yo' shit back, yo." She snatched his cellular out of his hand and pressed it to her ear. "Who am I speaking with? What up, Abdullah? This Octavia." She listened to what he had to say before responding. "Yeah, I got 'em right here. Nothing. Sitting here looking stupid." She listened again. "Cool. You know the place. Just remember to bring that bag wit'chu, king. Awright, boo." Octavia disconnected the call and tossed the cell phone aside. Pinning her gun on Jabari, she got dressed with one hand and then instructed him to get dressed. "Be easy, nigga. You make any sudden moves and that's yo' ass."

Jabari mugged Octavia the entire time he was getting dressed. He called her every insulting name he could think to call a woman of her size.

"Be sure to throw paid in there too, sweetie," Octavia told him. "With the loot I'm finna get off these Nigerian niggas, I'll be able to fly out to D.R. and get snatched like them Instagram model bitches," she assured him. "Then I'll be able to pull me a real baller - nothin' like yo' wannabe dope boy ass."

"I knew I shoulda never fucked wit'cho fat ass," Jabari said through squared jaws. He balled his fists and kicked at the floor. In that moment, he wished he could bend over and kick his own ass.

Sanka was one of them niggas that insisted on knowing all of his acquaintances' residences, relationships, associates, and fuck buddies. What Jabari didn't know was Sanka had sunk his claws into Octavia long ago. He had Abdullah and Hakim approach her with a business proposal. She'd receive a manila envelope of five-thousand dollars a month just to keep them informed on what Jabari was doing. With that chunk of change, plus the bread Jabari was hitting her with to stash guns, drugs, and whatever else at her crib, she was living life on Easy Street. Although she'd fallen in love with Jabari, she knew deep down inside he didn't give a fuck about her. The nigga was selfish and only cared about what she could do for him. Every man she'd fooled around with sexed her and acted like they didn't know her when they saw her in the hood. This was all because she was a big girl. Octavia was tired of that shit though. She wanted a change, and she knew the only way she'd get it was by getting plastic surgery and bagging herself a millionaire.

Awright, march yo' ass into the dining room," Octavia ordered, swaying her gun toward the living room and then picking up her treasure chest of sex toys.

"I can't believe this shit, son," Jabari fumed under his breath. "This fat bitch done sold ya boy out for lipo and a fuckin' BBL."

"Hurry the fuck up!" She kicked him in his butt. He righted himself before he could fall.

Jabari walked out of the bedroom with Octavia on his heels, holding him at gunpoint. She made him sit down in a chair at the kitchen table. Kneeling down, she unlocked the pink, sapphire-studded treasure chest and lifted its lid. Inside there were dildos of various sizes, butt-plugs, a cat-o-nine tails, and black leather masks among other things. Octavia removed two pairs of pink fur handcuffs and tossed them at Jabari's feet. She instructed him to cuff his wrists to each of the arms of the chair. He looked at her defiantly. She leveled her piece at his crotch and he felt queasy.

"Nigga, you don't scare me. I'm the bitch with the gun," Octavia reminded him. "Now do like I said 'fore I blow that big mu'fucka off. Ya heard?"

Jabari took a deep breath, picked up the handcuffs, and cuffed himself to the arms of the chair. Octavia pulled up a chair and sat a few feet away from him. She glanced at the clock on the wall then focused her attention back on Jabari. "Now we play the waiting game."

Chapter 14

A few minutes later, Octavia found herself ogling Jabari while he sat in the chair. She admired his full set of lips, recalling how many times she orgasmed from him eating her pussy alone. Her eyes wandered down to the bulge below his waist and she thought about all their sexual encounters. She couldn't front. Out of all the niggas she'd bedded, he was the best she ever had. His old thuggish ass knew her body nearly as well as she did. There were times she'd get off by the mere thought of him. He had her body under a spell. Shorty knew without a shadow of a doubt that once he was dead, she was going to miss that dick.

Octavia looked up to see Jabari smiling devilishly at her. He licked his bottom lip and gave her that sexy look he gave her right before her gave her the fuck of her life.

"I know what'chu thinking shorty," Jabari began in a sensual voice. "You gon' miss 'em, huh?"

Octavia looked at him like "Whatever, nigga" and waved him off.

"Well. Monster gon' miss you too." he confessed. "Check this out. I know nine times outta ten these African muthafuckas are gon' kill me, so how about, uh, you come ride this thang for old times' sake, huh?" Octavia stared at his crotch while rubbing her chin and thinking about his proposition. "If not for yourself, then for me, ma. Grant a nigga this one last request before he journeys into the unknown. That's the least you can do."

"Awright, fuck it." Octavia shot up in her chair. She switched hands with her gun and unzipped her jeans. Once she pulled them down, she spat in her hand and started manipulating her love button. Her pussy was warm to her touch and had already lubricated itself. Her eyes flickered as she leaned her head back. She held her mouth open in pleasure. Then she started moaning erotically. Her sexual calls turned Jabari on. He bit down on his bottom lip, and his dick was already threatening to break free of its denim prison.

Octavia's womanly scent invaded the air. Jabari loved it! Closing his eyes, he tilted his head back and took a deep breath. A smile spread across his lips. He looked down at his crotch and he'd pitched a tent in his jeans.

"Come on, ma. Ya boy ready to go, look at 'em." Jabari nodded down at his bulge.

When Octavia glanced down at his bulge and she got even wetter. She couldn't wait to ride him to a screaming orgasm.

"Damn, pa, the more I think about it, I really am gonna miss that dick," Octavia admitted. Removing her glistening fingers from her sex, she walked up on Jabari and wiped her essence below his nose. He closed his eyes and inhaled again. The biggest smile spread across his face. She then stuck her fingers inside his mouth and he sucked on them like they were dripping chocolate. "How that taste?"

"Good. Real good." He sucked on his lips and licked them. "Now, take Monster outta his cage and saddle 'em up." *Yeah, bitch, walk yo' hoe-ass right into this Venus flytrap,* Jabari thought. As soon as he saw his opening to turn the odds in his favor, he was going to take it and make her wish she never betrayed him.

"Okay, daddy," Octavia replied. She faked like she was about to unzip his jeans and whacked him upside the head with her pistol. A bloody gash opened on the side of his head and ran down the side of his face. He looked around discombobulated before falling unconscious. His head hung to his chest and he snored loudly. "Silly rabbit, tricks are for kids."

Octavia knew Jabari was plotting to flip the script on her. Over the years, she became real acquainted with his ticks. She could tell he was planning his escape by his wandering eyes. Octavia pulled up her jeans and zipped them back up. Exhaling, she sat back down in her chair, glanced at the clock on the wall, and waited for Abdullah to arrive.

***

"Uhhhhhhh!" Jabari groaned like a shambling zombie as he regained consciousness. He had a migraine the size of Manhattan and the blood on the side of his face had dried. He could hear a

94

couple of people conversing as he tried to focus his blurry vision. He blinked his eyes repeatedly. Slowly, his vision came back to him. He saw Abdullah and Octavia standing at the kitchen counter. She was running her fee for capturing him through a money counter. Beside the Gucci knapsack she was feeding the money counter from was the duffle bag of drugs he'd acquired from his safe. Seeing her with his bag of merch infuriated him. He was so irate he squared his jaws and tried to snatch his wrists free of his restraints. The noise from his ruckus drew the attention of Octavia, Abdullah, and his African hitters.

"It's about time yo' bitch ass woke up, nigga." Abdullah smiled wickedly, making his way over to him with Hakim by his side.

"We told the boss you were the one behind kidnapping his niece, and he wasn't even shocked," Hakim told him. "He said outta all of the ones he made his proposal to, he knew you'd be the one to buck the system."

"Yeah. He said you're too stubborn and prideful," Abdullah chimed in. "He hoped that you wouldn't do what came natural to you, but if you did, he wasn't at all worried."

"Nope. And that's because he had a contingency plan," Hakim added with a wicked smile. He tapped his finger against his temple. "Boss is a smart man. A really smart man."

Jabari snorted up the biggest, nastiest loogie he could and spit in Hakim's face. "Fuck the both of you bitches!"

Hakim's face balled up angrily and he wiped the nasty glob off his cheek. He upped his gun to blow out Jabari's brain, but Abdullah stepped in front of him. "Relax. Sanka wants 'em alive. And that's how I intend to bring 'em back."

"Fuck that! This piece of shit spit in my face," Hakim said through clenched teeth and cocked the hammer back on his piece.

"Okay," Abdullah told him and stepped out of his path. "But you know what happens to those who disobey orders. They wind up on his shit list, and when that happens, we're sent after them." He allowed what he said to roll around in his partner's head before he continued. "Now I love you like we came outta the same womb, but

I will not let you get in the way of my duty, especially not when it's gettin' in the way of me feeding my family."

Hakim knew how relentless Sanka was when it came to making one of his hands pay for being insubordinate, and he didn't want that kind of hellstorm coming down upon him. Hakim took a deep breath, uncocked the hammer of his pistol, and stashed it inside of his waistband.

Hakim pointed his crooked finger at Jabari. "You are one lucky Akata, you know that?"

"Boss said he wants 'em brought back alive, but he didn't say anything about us not whipping his ass." Abdullah smirked with his hand on his shoulder.

Hakim smiled devilishly and rubbed his hands together. "That's right. He didn't, did he?"

Abdullah looked over his shoulder and motioned the African hitters over to them. "Gentlemen, put away your pistols. It's time we give Mr. Jabari a good ol' fashioned ass whoopin'."

"And that's my cue to leave," Octavia said under her breath. "Awright, Abdullah, we're straight here. I'm gonna be on my merry way now."

Abdullah didn't bother looking back at Octavia when he waved her off. Octavia grabbed both bags, slipping the strap of one of them over her shoulder. She opened the front door and took one last look back at Jabari.

"Man, all that good dick goin' to waste." Octavia shook her head pitifully before walking out of the door. She locked the door behind her and walked towards her car.

Jabari stared down the African hitters as they poured inside of the kitchen. They were anxious to get a piece of his trifling ass. If there was anyone in the world that deserved the beating he was about to get, it was him.

"You fuck-boys do yo' worst. I'm built for this shit." Jabari mugged them, looking around at all of their faces.

"With pleasure!" Hakim snarled, kicking him square in the mouth and sending blood flying everywhere.

Jabari fell backwards in his chair with busted lips and a bloody grill. He winced as the Africans attacked him like a school of piranhas. They punched, kicked, stomped, and hit him with different appliances in the kitchen. Jabari tried to fight them off, but his efforts were useless. The Africans proved to be entirely too much for him. The last thing he recalled was a blender slamming into the side of his head and then everything went black.

***

Jabari sat between two of the African hitters as they were driving in a triple black Lincoln Navigator. The enormous vehicle was eerily quiet with each man being consumed by their own thoughts. Jabari stared at his monstrous reflection in the passenger window. He had a bloodied, swollen face and his left eye was shut. On top of that, he was missing two front teeth and spitting bloody loogies every five to ten minutes.

Abdullah threatened to put Jabari's dick in a blender if he didn't give up Sankeesy's whereabouts. The thought of having his meat chopped up into dog food made him queasy, but he held fast to his gangsta. The Africans had to salute his G. A lesser man would have folded under all that pressure, but Jabari held it down. He told them niggas the only way he'd tell them where Sankeesy was stashed was if he could ride along with them. They reluctantly agreed, so here he was now going along for the ride.

Jabari wasn't the slightest bit worried about Jibbs' and Spank's welfare. He already had a system set up for them to know if their plan had gone left. They had two different ways of knocking at the door so either of them would know what was up. The first way of knocking was to let the other know what was good. The second way of knocking was to let the other know shit had hit the fan and it was time to get on some certified head-busting shit. Jabari figured if his hitters could knock down most of Sanka's soldiers, then maybe they would have a fighting chance. As of now he was brainstorming a way to get out of this mess in one piece.

"Make a right up here at this corner." Jabari nodded his directive, unable to move his hands. The pink fur handcuffs kept his wrists restrained so he couldn't move his hands.

"Which house?" Abdullah asked from the front passenger seat. His attention was focused out of the passenger window searching for the crib they were looking for.

"Three houses down, to yo' right," Jabari told him. "It's dilapidated. All white. You can't miss it."

The Lincoln Navigator pulled four houses away from the crib Sankeesy was holed up in. The second Navigator harboring the other African hitters pulled up in front of it. The SUV's turned off and everyone began checking their guns to make sure they were fully loaded.

"You guys stay where you are until I give you the word," Adebisi told his squad through his ear piece. He then turned around to Jabari in the back seat. "Once you reach the back door, is there a certain way you knock so they'll know it's you?" Jabari turned to the passenger window and showed him the coded knock he and his hitters used. Adebisi made a mental recording of it so he wouldn't forget it. "Awight then. Adebisi, Mandla, y'all stay here and keep a close eye on this fucka. If he tries anything, you put one between his eyes. The rest of you come with me."

Abdullah contacted the other Africans in the truck in front of them and let them know they were going to make their move. Everyone hopped out of the Navigators to storm the house.

Chapter 15

"I gotta piss," Jabari told Mandla, shaking his leg impatiently. "Yeah? Well, go right in yo' pants," Mandla replied. "You one cold-ass African." Jabari retorted. "A'ight then. After I piss in this overgrown porta potty, I'ma shit right behind it."

"Go right ahead." Mandla called his bluff.

"Oh, you think a nigga bullshitting? Okay." Jabari was about to deliver on his threat until Adebisi interrupted.

"Mandla, take this guy somewhere he can piss, shit, or whatever," Adebisi ordered. "I just got this truck washed and detailed. The last thing I want is him putting his stink in it."

"I know you're not falling for this crap!" Mandla said. "This Akata more than likely has a trick up his sleeve."

"Maybe so. But what good are his tricks when you're the man with the gun, aye?" Adebisi asked over his shoulder. "If he tries anything, you put a hole in his thinker and leave 'em right where he stands."

Mandla took a deep, exasperated breath before hopping out of the Navigator and walking around to the other side of it. He snatched the back door open and grabbed Jabari out of it roughly. He pressed his gun into Jabari's kidney and spoke into his ear.

"You heard 'em. You try me, and you'll come back reincarnated as a butterfly."

Annoyed, Jabari sucked his teeth and rolled his eyes. "Mannn, I gotta use the john, ain't nobody runnin' game on you niggas."

"You better not." Mandla shoved him forward with his gun. His eyes swept over the block, looking for somewhere for Jabari to answer nature's call. He spotted a yellow house with a "For Sale" sign on its front lawn. Its lights were out and there was no car in the driveway, so he figured there wasn't anyone home. "Okay. We're going to that house over there with the for sale sign on the front lawn." He nodded at the house he had in mind.

Mandla shoved Jabari in the direction of the house and escorted him there at gunpoint.

***

The African hitters invaded the yard of the house where Sankeesy was being held hostage. Guns out, they moved stealthily with every intention of shooting to kill. Swaying his hand here and there, Abdullah gave the hitters the areas of the house to post up. Once they followed his commands, he walked up on the back porch and pressed his ear against the door. He didn't hear anything on the other side of the door, so he knocked on it the way Jabari had shown him. He held his gun down at his side and surveyed his surroundings. The African hitters were on point and ready. He waited a while longer before knocking on the back door again in the way he'd been shown. A second later, he got the surprise of a lifetime.

Blocka, blocka, blocka, blocka!

Bullets punctured holes through the back door, taking Abdullah off his feet. He crashed to the ground, wincing. Right after, the Africans returned fire, sending pieces of the iron door flying everywhere. Abdullah massaged his chest under his life-saving bulletproof vest and threw up his hand for them to fall back.

"Stop firing! Stop firing! You might..." Abdullah winced from his sore chest. "You might hit Sankeesy."

The gunfire ceased and gunsmoke wafted around those that had been shooting. With the assistance of two of the Nigerians, Abdullah was helped back onto his feet. He waved the men off so they'd release him and let him take control of the matter. The Nigerians let go of him and he crept up on the back door cautiously. Gripping his gun with both hands, he pressed his back against the side of the ruined back door and called out to the shooter.

That muthafuckin' Jabari set us up, Abdullah thought, wincing and rubbing his sore chest underneath his body armor. *I'ma kill that cocksucka as soon as I get Sankeesy back.*

"We don't want any trouble!" Abdullah told them. "Just give us the girl back and we'll leave here peacefully. You have my word."

"Abdullah?" Sankeesy called out.

Abdullah frowned. "Sankeesy? Is that you?"

"Yeah."

100

"Sanka sent us to get you. Are you awright?"

"Yes. How about you?"

"Besides being shot a second ago, I'm okay."

"Oh my God! I'm so sorry, Abdullah," Sankeesy told him. She was extremely apologetic. "Jibbs and I thought you were coming to harm us."

"Jibbs?" Abdullah frowned confusingly. He looked back at the Africans and they shrugged. They didn't know who the fuck Jibbs was either. "Sankeesy, who the hell is Jibbs?"

Sankeesy gave Abdullah a quick rundown of everything that had transpired in his absence. Including Jibbs' involvement in her kidnapping and then his role in saving her from Spank's serial rapist ass. Sankeesy agreed to leave with Abdullah, but only if Jibbs could come along and they promised not to harm him. Abdullah agreed, but had to get the okay from Sanka. He hit him up and explained everything. He was cool with it.

"Awright. We're all good," Abdullah told Sankeesy before putting his burnout away.

"You sure?" Sankeesy asked.

"Yes. Sanka gave the okay."

"Awright. We're gonna come out now."

"Abdullah, look!" one of the Nigerians pointed to the basement window. When he looked, he saw smoke escaping from the window.

"Sankeesy, what the hell is going on in there? I see smoke," a frowning Abdullah asked.

"That's the asshole that raped her, bruh," Jibbs spoke up. "I took care of 'em. This whole place is gonna go up, so it's best we get outta here, fast."

"Okay. Come on out," Abdullah told them. He jumped down from the back porch and joined the others on the lawn.

"I know we're not going to let this Akata walk without wetting 'em up," one of the Africans whispered into Abdullah's ear.

Abdullah shook his head no. "Sanka is allowing 'em to keep his life. Besides, if it wasn't for him, Sankeesy would be dead." The African wasn't happy about letting Jibbs slide for his participation in kidnapping Sankeesy, but if Sanka gave the order to leave him be, then he didn't have any choice but to fall back.

The back door slowly opened. Sankeesy emerged holding Jibbs' hand. They were both holding guns, but he had the straps of the bags of stolen drug money over his shoulders. Abdullah zeroed in on the duffle bags in Jibbs possession. Jibbs picked up on his wandering eye instantly. He already knew what was to come next.

"Is that the money from the Dominican spots y'all hit?" Abdullah asked him.

Jibbs nodded in response. "Yep. Sho' is."

"Hand it over," the African beside Abdullah said, motioning for him to toss him the duffle bags.

"No can do, homeboy. You see, I have this thing where when I take a nigga's shit, I don't give it back." Jibbs mugged all of the African hitters standing out there on the lawn. Though he had love for Sankeesy, his heart wasn't as soft as marshmallows. He was still a gangsta. He felt like coming up off those bags would be like chopping off his nutsack and handing it to them. *I swear on God and Heaven, shit gon' get real nasty 'fore these fools get these bags.*

Feeling the tension thickening between both sides, Sankeesy stepped in front of Jibbs to shield him from any exchange of gunfire. She took her gun into both hands and spread her legs. She was prepared to start splitting wigs if it came to that.

Jibbs' forehead wrinkled when she stepped in front of him. He knew she was willing to sacrifice her life to save him, and that melted his heart. Still, what kind of man would he be if he were to allow her to do such a thing?

"Nah, ma, I'ma hold it down," Jibbs said, passing her the duffle bags of drug money and taking her gun. He put himself in between Sankeesy and the army of angry Africans. "If this shit gets outta hand, take that loot and get the fuck outta New York, and don't look back."

Tears twinkled in Sankeesy's eyes as she stared up at Jibbs. She'd never been with a man that showed so much compassion and affection for her. Although they were in the face of danger right then, she felt so loved and protected by him. She knew it was crazy, or maybe it was that Stockholm Syndrome she heard about, but either way, she couldn't help how she felt. She was in love with Jibbs.

"I know this might sound crazy, but I love you, Jibbs," Sankeesy confessed.

Jibbs, who had both his guns pinned on the Africans, couldn't believe his ears. What was even crazier was that he felt the same way about her, but he was trying to deny it because they didn't know each other that well. Keeping his eyes on the Africans, he glanced over his shoulder and replied. "I love you too, shorty, now get outta—"

Sankeesy turned his face toward her and kissed him deeply. Jibbs kept both his guns and one eye on the Africans.

Sankeesy kissed him one more time on the lips. She smiled with love sparkling in her eyes. "I don't care what happens tonight. I'm never leaving you—ever."

Abdullah saw the Africans on either side of him about to make a move on Jibbs. He made eye contact with them and shook his head. They all wanted blood that night, but they knew the consequences behind them going against his orders would be severe.

"Look, if you want to hold onto that money, fine. It doesn't make any difference to me," Abdullah assured Jibbs. "But we needa get the hell outta here before the police get here." He glanced up at the house. He could smell the smoke in the air and hear the crackling of the fire.

Jibbs continued to hold his Glizzies on the Africans while Sankeesy held him from behind. He mulled over what Abdullah said to him in his mind over and over again until he finally made up his mind. Taking a deep breath, he put the hammers of his pistols back in place and lowered them to his sides.

Jibbs nodded and said, "Okay. Let's g—"

The sound of gunfire startled everyone in the backyard. Abdullah ran out of the backyard, motioning for his African hitters to follow him. They all fell in step behind him. Jibbs and Sankeesy followed closely behind them.

They made it to the front of the house in time to see the Navigator speeding away. They looked out into the street and saw

Adebisi laid out with his top missing. At this time, police car sirens blared from afar and were quickly closing in on their location.

"Son of a bitch. Come on!" Abdullah motioned for them to follow him. They climbed into the other Navigator. The driver fired it up and sped away in the opposite direction Jabari had gone.

***

Mandla ushered Jabari down the gangway and into the back of the house. He located a dark corner for Jabari to relieve himself. He stood counter-clockwise to him, holding him at gunpoint.

"Go ahead. Take your leak," Mandla told him. "But be forewarned, should you pull anything out of your zipper other than your dick, I'm going to send something hot through the back of your head. Do you copy?"

"Yeah. I got'chu." Jabari replied nonchalantly. Handcuffed, he unzipped his jeans and pulled out his meat. A look of relief came across his face, releasing the pressure from his bladder.

Blocka, blocka, blocka, blocka!

Gunfire cut through the silence of the night and stole Mandla's attention. His face balled up as he listened closely for the shots again. Jabari's neck craned around his shoulder. Mandla was distracted. This opened a window of opportunity and he was going to take advantage of it. Jabari swung around and kicked the gun out of Mandla's hand. He entangled the chain of his handcuffs around Mandla's wrist. Then he jumped up, wrapping his legs around his neck, and forced him to the ground. Jabari held his arm as tight as he could. Using his thighs, he applied pressure around his neck, cutting off his oxygen. Gagging and coughing, Mandla tried desperately to pry Jabari's thighs from around his neck, but his efforts failed. Blood clots formed in the whites of his eyes and the veins on his forehead threatened to burst under the extreme pressure.

Jabari clenched his teeth as sweat ran down his face. The veins on his temples and hand bulged as he choked the life out of Mandla. Shortly, the Nigerian went as limp as a wet noodle in his grasp and released his last breath. Jabari held him for a while longer before letting him go. He ran through his pockets until he came up with the handcuff key and a cellular phone. He unlocked the metal bracelets, removed them, and recovered the gun he'd kicked out of Mandla's hand. He stole one last look at Mandla's lifeless body as he fled from the backyard of the house.

Ghost & Tranay Adams

Chapter 16

The gunfire coming from the house where Sankeesy was held hostage put Adebisi on high alert. He kept his piece close to him and became more aware of his surroundings. He started to hop out to see if niggas were straight, but figured it was best to hold it down. For all he knew, Abdullah and them could come running back to the truck for a fast getaway. He didn't want the fault of them being caught falling upon his shoulders, so he convinced himself to stay put.

Adebisi stretched his arms and yawned like he was waking up early in the morning. That wasn't the case though. He'd been up the past two days handling business for Sanka and squeezing in quality time for his wife and kids. Needless to say, Adebisi was tired as shit and couldn't wait to get back home to his bed. Thinking about his family brought a crooked grin to his lips and his eyes involuntarily closed. His head would drop, but he'd throw it back up. He was fighting his sleep but his efforts would prove useless in the end.

"Psssst! Psssst!" Someone called for Adebisi's attention.

His eyes fluttered back open and he looked over his shoulder out of the window. His eyes widened fearfully when he saw Jabari standing outside with a gun aimed at him. Adebisi went to take a shot at him ,but unfortunately the driller had the drop on him. Jabari pulled the trigger of his pistol twice. The first bullet struck Adebisi right between the eyes while the second one struck him directly in the forehead, launching his head backwards. His blood and brain fragments splattered on the dashboard.

Jabari opened the driver's door from inside the Navigator and pulled Adebisi's body out into the street. He slid into the driver's seat and slammed the door behind him. He cranked the truck up and plucked pieces of brain from the dashboard. A disgusted look was on his face as he tossed the bloody pieces out of the window. He put the truck in drive and sped away from the curb.

Jabari raced up the street, dialing up Monty on Mandla's cell phone. Now that Sanka had found out he was the one behind his spots being hit and Sankeesy's kidnapping, he didn't see any reason for his best friend's blood to be spilt.

"Come on, son. Pick up, pick up, pick up," Jabari said, antsy, glancing in the side view mirror to see if those African niggas were on him. They weren't. "Fuuuuck, Blood! Shit!" he cussed when neither Monty or Bogus answered their jacks. The thought of Scorpion having Paperchase in his possession crossed his mind, so he hit him up. He couldn't keep from smiling when he finally answered.

"'Sup, big homie? I was just callin' to see if you got ahold of baby bro yet?"

Scorpion's reply instantly made Jabari glassy-eyed. He disconnected the call and tossed the cell phone on the passenger seat. He pulled over on the side of the road and threw the Navigator in park. He gripped the steering wheel with both hands and bowed his head. His shoulders rocked as he proceeded to cry and bang his fist against the dashboard. His lowdown selfish ass cried like a bloody, slimy newborn baby pulled out of its mother's womb.

Jabari's guilt came down on him like a ton of bricks. He wanted his day-one homie dead so he could level up to boss status, but everything had blown up in his face. Not only had he lost the truest friend he'd ever had, but his dream of securing a plug on the best dope money could buy and ruling the streets of New York had gone out of the window. Now he didn't have jack shit. And on top of that, his man's death was weighing heavily on his mind.

A nigga can still get thangs to movin' and shakin' on his own. I gotta couple of connects and favors I can call in to get my hands on some dope. The shit may not be Rebirth quality, but if it's pure enough, I can cut it to somethin' decent and turn a nice li'l profit every week, Jabari thought, staring up at the ceiling with tears leaking from his eyes. *Hell yeah. That's exactly what cha boy gon' do. Whether it's coke, dope, weed, or pills, I'ma be the man in one of these lanes.*

Jabari patted himself down hoping Abdullah's men didn't take what little dope he had to get his mind right. His bloody, busted lips formed a smile when he felt what he was looking for in the small pocket of his jeans. He pulled what looked like an aglet of cocaine from his small pocket and stared at it like it was a flawless diamond. He took a bump up his right nostril and laid his head back against the headrest. His glassy eyes twinkled and he swallowed the drip at the back of his throat. Feeling his nose beginning to leak, he snorted and wiped it with his finger.

Jabari took the time to pull himself together before picking his cell phone back up. He hit up the young nigga Ramone and made plans to link up. They agreed to meet at Toya's crib, which was okay with him. All he wanted to do was break the news of Paperchase being killed and run down his new plans of taking over the city. He didn't have any doubts of little homie not being down. He was young, hungry, ambitious, and didn't mind pulling a trigger for the good of the cause.

Jabari took one more bump from the aglet and pulled on his nose. He then cranked up the Navigator and drove away. The backlights of his truck disappeared into the night.

***

Rusting barrels of burning shards of wood were scattered throughout the warehouse, with embers floating around the open fires like wasps. The burning aroma invaded the atmosphere and made it nearly impossible to breathe. The smell didn't bother Scorpion in the slightest though. The flames of one particular barrel seemed to have Scorpion under its hypnosis. He stood in front of it, holding a brown leather travel bag with both hands. The ends of his duster flapped behind him with every gust of wind that flowed through the old building.

A thousand thoughts ran rampant through Scorpion's mind while the fire held him under its spell. He never thought in a million years his lifestyle would lead to him having to bear arms against his brother. Had he had knowledge of this, he would have never participated in street-life in the first place. A part of him wanted to say fuck it and let his younger brother slide. But the gangsta in him wanted to hold a grudge and show his sibling no one was above the consequences that came from betraying a street legend.

Scorpion knew within his heart that if he didn't smash his brother, he'd lose the respect of the streets, and niggas would be trying him left and right. On the other hand, if he did smash him for the violation, his death would weigh heavily on his conscience and he may not be able to live with himself. He was in a damned if he did, damned if he didn't situation. No matter the choice he made, he was sure it would affect his life for as long as he was above ground.

"Fuck it, Dunn! That nigga threw his life away the day he stuck his dick in my bitch," Scorpion thought out loud. "Now he's gotta man up and deal with the consequences. Bruh knows how this shit go."

Scorpion switched hands with the travel bag to answer his ringing cell phone. "What up, Blood?" he answered the call. "A'ight. Here I come now."

Scorpion hung up and raised the shutter. He stood aside, watching the Mercedes-Benz truck back inside. Once the SUV was inside, he lowered the shutter and approached the back of it. Bogus and Monty jumped out of the truck, slamming their doors behind them and walking to the hatch of the vehicle.

"Blaat!" Monty greeted Scorpion, shaking up with him.

"Blaat!" Bogus greeted him and shook up with him as well.

"So, I take it he's in there." Scorpion threw a finger up at the hatch.

"Yep. I take it our bread is in there." Monty pointed at the leather bag.

"The entire fifty bands, young homie," Scorpion replied.

"A'ight. Now that's what a nigga love to hear." Monty grinned before popping open the hatch of the Mercedes-Benz truck.

Paperchase mugged the three of them while he lay gagged and bound. The side effects of the tranquilizer darts had worn off just before he'd made it to the warehouse.

Get this nigga up out this muthafucka, B," Scorpion told them with a sway of his hand.

Bogus and Monty grabbed hold of each one of Paperchase's legs and yanked him out of the back of the SUV. He hit the ground so hard he knocked the wind out of his lungs. His face balled up tightly and he rocked from side to side.

"That's for being a disloyal-ass bitch!" Monty spat on him.

Bogus cocked his leg back and kicked Paperchase in the stomach. It looked like he was trying to kick a field goal. Paperchase's eyes watered; he was in so much pain. That kick made it feel like he was going to shit his pants.

"That's for putting smut on the gang," Bogus told him.

Scorpion passed the leather travel bag to Monty. Unzipping it, he smiled upon seeing all the blue faces it contained. He allowed Bogus to take a look and he smiled too. After Monty zipped up the bag, he and Bogus shook up with Scorpion and drove out of the warehouse.

Scorpion let down the shutter and made his way towards Paperchase. Still wincing from the assault, he lay on his side, watching his brother approach. Scorpion pulled off his duster and tossed it aside. Reaching at the small of his back, he drew two big ass machetes. Paperchase could see his reflection in them. He knew his life was coming to an end and he'd be damned if he pleaded to keep it.

Paperchase squeezed his eyes closed, bracing himself for the first strike of the machete. It never came. Instead, Scorpion sliced off his gag and his bondages. Paperchase looked at him with confusion written across his face. He was even more perplexed when he tossed one of the machetes beside him.

"I'ma give you a gangsta's death, li'l bruh," Scorpion told him, his slightly hairy chest rising and falling with every breath. "You've definitely earned it, Slime."

Paperchase tried to read his brother's true intentions, but failed miserably. Not sure if Scorpion was playing a trick on him, he hesitantly reached for the machete lying next to him. Once he had it in his grasp, he jumped to his sneakers and prepared for battle.

"Yeaaah. That's what I'm talkin' 'bout, li'l nigga." Scorpion smiled wickedly and did fancy maneuvers with the machete. It was obvious he was well-trained in handling the blade.

"This what'chu want, big bruh? Fuck it! Let's get to it, Dunn." Paperchase showed off his skills with the machete. His battle cry resonated within the four walls of the tenement as he charged at him, lifting his machete above his head.

Scorpion released his battle cry, charging at him a second later and lifting his machete above his head. The flames of the burning barrels of wood danced in the air as they ran past them. The distance between them was closing drastically.

Scorpion and Paperchase swung their machetes at the exact same time. As soon as the blades clashed, sparks flew in both directions. They went at it like savages in the machete fight, becoming hot and sweaty, neither willing to give up the good fight. Grunts and even screams were exchanged as both men suffered from cuts of each other's machete. The fight seemed about even until Scorpion got in his bag.

Scorpion ducked the wild swings of Paperchase's machete. Coming back up, he backhand punched his brother and made him stumble backwards. Before he could regain his balance, Scorpion was on his ass. Charging forward, he kicked Paperchase in the chest and sent him hurling back. Paperchase crashed into a number of barrels, causing them to spill their burning contents. Paperchase winced, lying among burning shards of wood and flying embers. He felt like a turkey trapped in an oven the day before Thanksgiving.

Paperchase scanned the area for his machete until he located it. He'd almost grabbed it when Scorpion kicked it out of his reach. He then kicked him in his side and he howled in pain. Next, he pressed his boot against his chest and placed the tip of his machete against the side of his neck. Instantly, a slither of blood ran from the tiny wound.

Chapter 17

"Go ahead! Do it! Finish it…finish it! I deserve it!" a teary-eyed Paperchase told him.

Scorpion, nostrils flaring, stared down at him. His eyes slowly swelled with tears as he thought back to all of the good and bad times he'd shared with his brother growing up. Tears broke down his cheeks unevenly and snot oozed out of his nose. "What are you waiting for, bruh? Do it! Handle yo' bidness, nigga!" Paperchase urged him. He was literally crying now - not because he was about to be killed but because he'd broken his brother's heart.

Still holding the machete to his side of his brother's neck, Scorpion wiped the wetness from his eyes. "I'm not gon' murk you, li'l bruh. If I were to kill you, it would kill me." He took the machete from Paperchase's neck and pulled him up.

Abruptly, Paperchase hugged his sibling brotherly-like. Tears burst from their eyes.

"I fucked up, bruh. I really fucked up," Paperchase's voice cracked. "I'm sorry I hurt chu, yo. Me and Liv shoulda never happened." He went on to tell him that Olivia was pregnant by some other nigga and that he'd gotten what he deserved fucking with her. "That shit was foul, son."

Scorpion held Paperchase by the back of his head and pressed his forehead against his. He held his gaze for a minute. Then he kissed him on his forehead and hung his arm around his neck.

"I wanna make shit right between us, Dunn," Paperchase told him. "Is there any possible way a nigga can do that? I'm all ears."

Thinking things over, Scorpion bowed his head and rubbed his chin. When he finally came up with something that could straighten things out between him and Paperchase, he addressed him.

"I want chu to gimme yo' plug's contact. Then I want you to pull together whatever loot chu got stashed and leave New York." Paperchase's eyes bugged. "You heard right. Leave NY and never return. Start your life over from scratch. No one will ever come after you. As far as the homies are concerned, you're already dead and buried."

Paperchase thought on it for a second, running his hand down his face. Looking back to Scorpion, he nodded his head in agreement. "A'ight. You got my word, yo. I'll leave."

"Tonight." Scorpion tossed him the key to his ride.

"Tonight." Paperchase caught the keys. He tossed him his extra cell phone and he caught that too.

"Now, about that Rebirth plug."

"Gimme yo' jack."

Paperchase took his brother's cellular. He had a photographic memory, so he memorized all the contacts stored in his cell phone. He programmed Sanka's digits into Scorpion's jack. Then he hit him up to make the introduction. Paperchase played the background while his big bro paced the floor chopping it up with Sanka, speaking in code so anyone listening wouldn't know what they were talking about. By the time they'd gotten off the phone, Scorpion was as happy as a pig in shit.

"We're good?"

"Everything is copacetic." Scorpion slapped hands with Paperchase and pulled him into his one armed embrace. He kissed him on the cheek then on the side of his forehead. "I love you, li'l nigga."

"I love you too, big bruh," Paperchase replied.

Scorpion, with one hand on his brother's shoulder, threw his head towards the entrance of the building. "Get outta here, Slime. My shit is parked at the back of this muthafucka. Cherry-red Beamer truck, sitting on them gold thangs."

"What about you, son? How you gon' raise up outta here?"

"I'ma hit up my people to slide through."

There was silence between the brothers. The only thing heard was the crackling of the shards of wood cooking inside of the rusted barrels.

Paperchase looked up at his brother with hopeful eyes. "Am I gonna see you again?"

"Fa sho'. Just hit me up once you get settled wherever you're going."

114

Paperchase nodded before speaking again. "A'ight."

Paperchase turned to walk away. Then he suddenly turned around and hugged his brother with one arm. He hugged him back with the arm of the hand he used to hold his machete. The brothers stayed locked in that moment for what seemed like an eternity to them. They shook up one last time and darted out of the tenement. Scorpion watched his back until he disappeared. His cell phone rang and he picked it right up. He was surprised to hear Jabari's voice on the other end. He didn't waste any time asking him about his brother. "Li'l bruh's gone on a long vacation. Yep." He disconnected the call. Then he hit up his "People".

***

Paperchase pulled off the grounds of the warehouse. He hadn't been gone five minutes and he already missed his brother and New York. He and the homies made their living hustling on these very streets. He'd shot, stabbed, robbed, stole and got his first piece of ass out here. He had mad memories during his time in Brooklyn, and he was going to be sure to cherish them. Although the times were long gone, they still remained inside of his heart.

Paperchase was a lot of things, but he wasn't stupid. He was a hundred percent sure it had been Jabari that set him up to be kidnapped. Like he'd told him before he'd left his crib, no one knew where he laid his head. So that meant that he was the one who gave up his location.

"I shoulda heard you hissing all along, you fucking snake." Paperchase shook his head, thinking about his two-timing homeboy. Before he shook the city, he wanted to ride up on him and put two in his melon, but he knew it was best he did like his brother told him.

Fuck 'em! I'll let these scandalous streets settle the score for me.

Stopping at a red traffic light, Paperchase searched the ashtray until he found a half of a blunt. He placed it between his lips and grabbed a Bic lighter. He was about to bring the flame to the tip of the bleezy when a realization smacked him like a broad that caught her man cheating. He was wide-eyed as the blunt fell from his lips in what seemed like slow-motion. The light had turned green, but he was left idling at the intersection.

"Muthafucka," Paperchase uttered, staring ahead at nothing.

It was that nigga that slept Jayshawn. It had to be! He bodied the young'un and framed me for his murder so Ramone would knock my shit back. That's why the li'l nigga was poppin' that shit earlier and challenged me to a gunfight.

"I can't believe this shit, Blood. Nigga was s'posed to be my man." Paperchase frowned, shaking his head.

Having memorized Ramone's number, he picked up the cell phone his brother gave him to holler at him.

***

Scorpion was as happy now that he had the Rebirth plug. Once he knocked down whomever the supplier wanted out of the way and secured a shipment, he was sure he'd have the city on lock. With the Woo under him, he had not only an army of head busters, but a street team capable of moving his work throughout the Big Apple.

"Yeah. A nigga about to be back on top like he's supposed to be, son." Scorpion smiled, licking his lips.

His cell phone's screen illuminated his face as he stared down at it. He didn't have any way to leave the warehouse since he'd given Paperchase his car. He didn't fuck with Ubers and taxis cost a nigga an arm and a leg, so they were out of the question. With that in mind, he hit up this broad named Lisa he'd connected with once he'd given Olivia's trifling ass her walking papers. He knew shorty from back in the day. She, Olivia, and him went to the same high school. She was on his nuts heavy back then, but his head was so far up Olivia's pussy she was practically invisible to him. He wound up linking back up with her when he saw her on a visit. Little mama was visiting her brother while Olivia and Paperchase were there to visit him. When he got back to the block, he got her number from her brother, and they'd been fucking with each other heavy ever since.

"Blood, where this broad at? She shoulda been here," Scorpion said to no one in particular and he texted homegirl who was supposed to pick him up on her Ducati.

Scorpion: *Yo, ma, where you @? It's cold asf out here.*

Lisa: *on the side of the building. Had 2 pee. My bad.*

Scorpion took a breath and pocketed his cell phone. He walked around to the side of the tenement, where he saw Lisa's lime green Ducati Supersport, but she wasn't anywhere to be found. His face balled up as he scanned the area, but couldn't find her.

Blood, this bitch bullshitting, and I'm tryna get the fuck up outta here, Scorpion thought. He cleared his throat and called out to shorty. "Lisa! Yo, Lisa! Where you at, shorty? I'm tryna leave this bitch in my rearview, ya dig?"

Hearing footsteps at his back, Scorpion went into killer mode and drew his piece. He turned around, ready to blast whomever it was trying to get the drop on him but stayed his trigger finger when he found Lisa. She was wearing her motorcycle helmet and white Air Force Ones. The sight of the gun made her throw her gloved hands up.

Scorpion sighed with relief seeing it was her. He tucked his gun in his waistband and gave her a hug. "Girl, you gotta be easy. You scared the shit outta the kid," he confessed. "I nearly blew your head off yo' shoulders, yo." Holding her about the waist, he stepped back to take a look at her. "Why don't chu take off that helmet and bless yo' man with a kiss."

Lisa nodded yes. She removed her motorcycle helmet and shook her dreadlocks free. Scorpion's eyes bugged when he laid eyes on not Lisa, but one of Sanka's African hitters. The dark-skinned Nigerian smiled wickedly and puckered up his big lips for a kiss. Scorpion mugged him as he went to draw his gun. He'd cleared it halfway out of his waistband when he felt a pinch at the side of his neck.

"Ow!" Scorpion's eyes bugged. He grabbed his neck with his other hand and turned around. Another African stood behind him holding a syringe and a pair of handcuffs. He lifted his pistol to shoot him as he tossed his handcuffs to the Nigerian standing behind him. Scorpion became light headed. His vision became cloudy. He saw a foursome of the man standing before him. He got off two shots. Both whizzed by the African's head and neck, narrowly missing him. Scorpion tried to take another shot, but his trigger finger wouldn't cooperate. His hand became limp and his gun slipped out of his hand. His eyes rolled to their whites and he collapsed to the ground.

The African that tossed the Nigerian handcuffs pulled out a black pillowcase. He thrashed it open as he walked towards his accomplice, who was handcuffing Scorpion's wrists behind him. He passed him the black pillowcase and he pulled it down over his head. The African tucked Scorpion's gun inside of his waistband. He looked ahead, whistled and motioned someone over. A second later, a white van was driving up and its sliding door was open.

Once Scorpion was loaded in the van, the Nigerians hopped inside and the driver pulled off. The van drove by the warehouse where Paperchase and Scorpion had the machete fight. The passenger window came down and a cell phone was thrown out of it. Slumped on the opposite side of the building was a cute, freckled face redbone with a mop of brown dreadlocks. She was wearing a hot pink bra and matching G-string. Her breasts rose and fell as she breathed easily. The Nigerians had ambushed shorty and injected her with the same sedative they had Scorpion.

Chapter 18

The moon shone marvelously in the cold night's sky and the crickets in the grass chirped obsessively. Drug addicts roamed the spooky streets looking for their poison of choice while dope boys kept an eye out for those looking to remedy their sickness.

Among those poor souls was Martha. She looked around aimlessly scratching like she had ants crawling all over her. She'd finished the ounce of Afghan heroin Jabari had laid on her days ago and now she needed some more to get herself right. She'd been blowing up Jabari's phone, but he wasn't answering her calls - or returning them, for that matter. Though she was hoping to get some more of that Afghan shit he had on deck, she wasn't aware of any dope boys pumping it, so she decided to return to the very avenue that had taken care of her since she'd become an addict.

Martha was scratching herself so intensely she wound up popping her scabs and causing them to bleed. When she looked at her hand, there was dead skin and blood caked underneath her fingernails. She wiped her hand on her jeans and walked up on a dope boy who'd just finished serving a fiend.

"What's the deal, ma? If you want it, I got it. If I don't have it, you don't want it. Ya heard?" The dope boy recited his slogan, snorting and then pulling on his nose.

"Yo, hook me up," Martha said, steadily scratching.

"I'll see what I can do. What'chu workin' wit', ma?" the dope boy replied, keeping his eye on the block.

"Nothing but I was hoping to get—"

"Bitch, you come up here looking for handouts? Get the fuck outta here, yo!" The dope boy scrunched up his face and waved her off. He spat to his right and looked back at her with recognition in his eyes. "Yo, shorty, don't I know you from somewhere?"

Recognition went off in Martha's eyes as well. She definitely knew the nigga. He was one of the two flunkies with Shakur The God the night he and Ramone brawled. Her heart skipped a beat. She knew that this encounter wouldn't end well, so she had to get the fuck out of there.

"N—no, I'm sorry you have me confused with someone else," Martha replied, throwing her hood on her head and walking away briskly.

"Yo, Shareef, who is that, God?" Rakeem asked with a frown, staring at Martha's back as she walked away. He was the other flunky that was with Shakur The God the night he and Ramone got busy.

"That's where I know that fiend from." Shareef snapped his finger, recalling who Martha was. He told Rakeem who Martha was before chasing after her, trying to wave her down. "Yo, shorty, come here for a minute yo, maybe we can work something out!"

Martha speed walked while glancing over her shoulder at him. She had a fear-streaked face. "No. That's o—that's okay."

"Yo, come here!" Shareef sprinted after her with Rakeem by his side.

Martha took off running, hearing their hurried footsteps growing closer behind her.

"Yo, stop that bitch, son!" Shareef hollered out to the fiends Martha was running past. They ignored his command, not wanting to get involved, but what he said next garnered their participation. "Yo, whoever snatches that bitch for me got three bags coming. Word is bond!"

Martha, who was now in a full sprint, looked over her shoulder, terrified, to see how close the dope boys were on her heels. Big fucking mistake! By the time she brought her head back around, a dope fiend wearing a backwards baseball cap and a fake dirty white mink coat stuck out his tattered sneaker. Martha tripped over his foot and slammed into the sidewalk. She lay there in agony with a pained expression on her face.

Shareef and Rakeem caught up with Martha and turned her over on her back. Shareef smiled seeing she was exactly who he thought she was. "Yeah, bitch, you thought we weren't gon' catch up wit'cho raggedy ass, huh?" Standing back up, he stomped her stomach, and when she grabbed herself, he kicked her in her back. She howled in pain.

"Ahem." The dopefiend rocking the backwards baseball cap cleared his throat.

"Pay the man, Keem," Shareef ordered Rakeem from over his shoulder while he turned Martha on her stomach and bound her wrists behind her back.

Rakeem hit the dope fiend's hand with the bags of heroin Shareef had promised, and he ran off somewhere to get high.

Shareef pulled Martha up to her feet roughly and Rakeem took her by her other arm. Shareef shoved his gun into her back and they walked her back up the block. To anyone watching, it looked like two soldiers bringing a prisoner of war back to their camp.

Four shooters hurried down the steps of a brownstone not too far from the spot Shareef was hustling. They mugged the entire block, looking for any niggas that posed a threat to their operation, but they didn't see anyone.

"Yo, God, what's the deal?" one of the shooters asked, pulling his hood off and revealing his bald head.

"This bitch owes a debt to the big homie. Y'all fools hold it down while we're gone," Shareef told them as he and Rakeem made their way across the street. They were headed to the brownstone where the top dawg resided.

Martha tried to yank and pull away from Shareef and Rakeem, but they held fast. Shareef pressed his pole into her back further and whispered into her ear.

"Check this out, bitch, you keep buckin' and I'ma leave yo' ass here in the middle of the fuckin' street, ya hemme?"

With that, Martha stopped trying to break their hold and went where they were taking her willfully.

Shareef and Rakeem walked up on the porch of the brown-stone and knocked. Shareef looked up and down the street for any police presence as they waited for someone to answer. They listened as the locks and chains were undone on the door. A second later, the front door was pulled open and they were standing before Shakur The God. He was wearing a black tank top, army green cargo pants, and Timbs. He looked menacing as shit with his dreadlocks hanging over his face. He took a bite of a juicy peach, munching on it as he waited to see what the fuck Shareef and Rakeem wanted.

"What up, black men?" Shakur The God asked. He hadn't noticed Martha yet because her head was bowed while Shareef and Rakeem were holding her up.

"Take a look at what we've got, God." Shareef smiled excitedly. Rakeem was smiling right along with him. They were both anxious to get the big homie's response.

Shakur The God switched hands with the peach. He grabbed Martha by her chin and lifted her face up. Her eyes bucked with fear once they met him, and he smiled wickedly.

"I knew we'd meet again," Shakur The God said. "Y'all bitches make yo'selves ghosts. These Gods and I have a li'l bidness to attend to," Shakur The God told the two bad bitches wearing black bikinis and aprons in his kitchen. They were passing a fat ass blunt of exotic weed between them while cooking up his favorite Jamaican dish.

As soon as Shakur The God gave his command, the women turned the fire off the pots, covered them, got dressed, and headed for the door. They kissed Shakur The God on each of his cheeks before disembarking the brownstone.

Shakur The God shut the door behind them and locked it. He threw his peach into the garbage can inside of the kitchen, grabbed a butcher knife out of the wooden block, and walked over to Martha while his flunkies held her up. He grabbed the end of her T-shirt and cut it straight up the middle. He slipped the butcher knife underneath her dingy bra, and slicked it upward. Instantly, her breasts popped out and sat back up. Though shorty was a straight clucker, somehow she maintained a decent body - minus the track marks and shit, of course.

Using the tip of the butcher knife, Shakur The God toyed with her nipples and watched sweat slide down her chest then over her tits. The terror in her eyes excited him to no end. He ran his tongue over his top lip and he felt his piece brick up in his pants.

"Now, I know you ain't got no money to pay that debt, but tonight the God aims to collect, so I'm willing to take other forms of payment," Shakur The God taunted, gently sliding the butcher knife down her torso and circling her navel. Martha's body tensed up, thinking he was about to plunge the knife into her belly. She tried to fight Shareef and Rakeem off once again, but she couldn't break their stronghold.

Shakur The God snatched the butcher knife from Martha's stomach and cracked her across the chin. Her head dropped and she went slack in Shareef and Rakeem's arms.

"What do you want us to do with her, son?" Rakeem asked.

"Drag that bitch down into the basement and tie her ass up, Keem," Shakur The God ordered him with a sway of his butcher knife. "Shareef, I want chu to break out the liquor and weed, then call some of the homies up. We're about to have ourselves a li'l party tonight."

Shareef, who'd just tucked his gun at the small of his back, smacked and rubbed his hands together. He knew exactly what the big homie was getting at, and he was all for it. Pulling out his cell phone, he hit up homie after homie inviting them to the "party".

***

Unbeknownst to Shareef and Rakeem, Martha's cell phone had slipped out of her pocket and landed in the middle of the street while they were escorting her to Shakur The God's brownstone. The old dopefiend Jabari had hit with the two hundred dollars to show him all of Sanka's trap houses had picked it up. He had planned on selling it until he saw a picture of Martha, Jayshawn, Chico, and Ramone on the lock screen. He knew then that Martha was Ramone's mother and she was in danger. He scrolled through the contacts in the cellular until he came upon Ramone's name. He hit him up and let him know what was going down.

The old dopefiend scratched under his chin as he listened to the phone ringing. As soon as Ramone answered, he reminded him who he was and told him what he'd seen.

"What? Are you sure?" Ramone asked heatedly.

"Yeah, youngsta, you needa get down here quick too. I don't know what these God Body niggas gon' do to yo' ol' girl," he told him, looking up at the address of the brownstone. At that very moment, the niggas Shareef had called up were walking up the steps of the brownstone for the party that was to take place. "Look, here, the address is—"

Once the dopefiend was sure Ramone had memorized the address, he told him he was going to post up and wait for him before hanging up. He then lurked in the shadows, watching and waiting, rubbing his hands to keep warm.

Chapter 19

Ramone hung up with the dopefiend and hipped Toya to what was going down. He gave her the address and she zipped through the streets. She blew through red lights and stop signs, not giving a fuck. Ramone didn't say a word. He wore the mask of a stone-faced killa as he checked the magazine of his pole to make sure it was fully loaded. He smacked it back inside of its handle and cocked it.

Ramone tooted coke up both of his nostrils, snorted, and pulled on his nose. His eyes were red-webbed and glassy. Little homie looked like a straight up psychopath like he did the very same night he tried to knock the brain out of that nigga Paperchase's head. He'd already lost his brother, so he would be damned if he lost his mother. Shakur The God and the rest of them Five Percenter niggas had him fucked up! They'd played with the wrong nigga's family, and to-night, they'd pay dearly for it.

Ramone focused his attention out of the passenger window, watching the streets past him in flickers of light. Toya bent a few corners and zipped up and down a couple of blocks before they were nearing their destination. They took in the scenery. The street that Martha had been kidnapped on looked like a real-life living hell. There were junkies coming to cop their drug of choice, leaving from getting it, or trying to proposition a dope boy to get some.

Toya couldn't help thinking how much some of the addicts with their pockmarked faces and arms looked like ghouls. If she didn't know any better, she'd swear a horror movie was being filmed on the block and the dopeheads were playing the monsters.

"What the fuck, babe? Look at them," Toya said, setting her gun in her lap and holding tight to it. Shit was looking so spooky there that she believed they'd come under attack from the dope-fiends.

"I see, baby. Shit's all fucked up down here, but fuck these fiends. We're here for my ol' girl," Ramone reminded her before hitting the dopefiend up that had called him earlier. He answered on the second ring and he asked him where he was.

"I'm right here, youngsta," Toya overheard him say. She and

Ramone looked ahead. The old dopefiend stepped out of the shadows, holding the cell phone to his ear with one hand and waving them down with the other.

"There he goes, ma. Pull up on 'em," Ramone told her. "We finna pull up now, my nigga." He hung up the cellular and pocketed it.

He and Toya jumped out of the car and approached the old dopefiend, who quickly gave him his mother's cell phone. He then gave him a full rundown of what had transpired in his absence and about all of the God Body niggas that had gone inside of Shakur The God's brownstone. He nodded across the street to the place. Its windows were lit from the lighting inside.

***

Martha stirred awake, wincing and groaning from the pain in her chin. Shakur The God had punched her so hard it felt like her bottom jaw had come unhinged. Her vision came into focus and she looked around the basement. She was surrounded by Shakur The God and all of his dope boys. They had their dicks sticking out of their zippers and were pumping them. Hungriness was in their eyes as they licked their lips and continued to jack themselves.

"The Gods have been waiting for you, Earth. We thought you'd never awake," Shakur The God said, wearing a sadistic smile across his lips. He was shirtless and his hairy chest was on full display. He had his dick in one hand and his gun down at his side in the other.

Martha's eyes bucked wide open and her heart was pounding so hard she thought it would explode inside of her chest. Looking down for the first time, she noticed she was completely naked and her hairy bush was exposed. Her head snapped to her left wrist, right wrist, left ankle, and right ankle. They were all bound by shackles, and the chains attached to them were bolted to the ceiling and the floor.

Martha took in the presence of all of the men again. There were ten of them in all, all shirtless, and all strapped like a Vietnam

126

platoon. Martha the lump of fear in her throat before addressing Shakur The God. "What—what do you p—plan on doing to me?"

Shakur The God slipped behind her, pressing his gun to the back of her head and whispering into her ear. "Me and the Gods are gonna fuck yo' ass in every single hole you've got, and when we finish, you and I our even." His breath was so hot against her earlobe it made it moist.

She was so terrified the hairs of her arms and legs stood up and a chill crawled up her back.

"You—you don't wanna do that. Trust—Trust me. I, uhhh—" Martha's eyes almost popped out of her face and her mouth flung open. Fire ripped through her asshole as Shakur The God shoved his pipe inside of her.

Shakur The God gripped her about the front of her and turned the side of her face to him. He scowled and spoke to her through clenched teeth. "Bitch, fuck what chu talkin' 'bout. You owe a nigga and you gon' pay a nigga tonight!" he grunted while holding her neck and wreaked havoc on her body, fucking her savagely.

She threw her head back, screaming at the top of her lungs as he pummeled her anus without regard to how she was feeling. Blood oozed out of her shit-locker, sliding down his stalk and then his nut-sack.

"Ahhhhh, fuck, fuck, fuuuck!" Martha screamed and screamed.

Shakur The God grunted as he punished her with long strokes. His hips clashed with her ample buttocks and the sound of skin slapping traveled throughout the basement.

"Ahhh, ahhh, ahhh, fuck, Grrrrrr," Martha squeezed her eyes shut, gritted, and hung her head. The veins covering her forehead and neck bulged, looking like they were going to pop. Her butthole felt like it had been torn open and splashed with alcohol.

"That's right, mama, take it, take it, take it, take it! Ummmm, unh, unh, unh!" Shakur The God grunted louder and louder, clutching her throat tighter. Her eyes watered and she turned red in the face. She lurched back and forth as she was getting struck from the back. Tears rolled down her cheeks and dropped off her chin.

"Yo, God, that bitch a champion!" one of the dope boys said, slapping five with one of the others.

"You ain't never lied, son!" another dope boy said.

"Man, big homie, let the rest of us getta taste of the broad," a third dope boy said, steadily stroking his dick.

Shakur The God removed his gun from Martha's head and pulled his pipe out of her ass. It was coated in dookie and blood. He set his gun upon the bar top, grabbed a few napkins, and started wiping his piece off. The dopeboy that was eager to fuck something darted past him, dropping his jeans around his ankles. He came up behind Martha and sunk his piece deep inside of her pussy. Her heat seared him up on entry and he shuddered, feeling her insides. He grabbed two handfuls of her breasts from behind and started pounding her out. It sounded like some nigga clapping mad hard down in the basement. Martha screamed and thrashed around while hanging from her shackles. The scene turned all of the dopeboys on, making them stroke their dicks faster and faster.

Shakur The God fastened his jeans, popped the top on a Heineken, and leant up against the bar. Every now and again he took a swig of his beer, watching his little homeboy pipe out Martha while holding his gun at his side.

"Unh, unh, unh!" the dopeboy grunted after busting deep inside of Martha. Wearing a smile on his face, he laid his hot, sweaty body against hers and panted, out of breath.

"Son, move yo' ass out the way." A second dope boy shoved him aside and he fell on the floor. He slid up in Martha, grabbed hold of her waist, and started beating her shit up from the back. The clapping sound started right back up again, only it was louder this time. The dope boys were barely out of their teens, so they were full of energy.

The dopeboys applauded their homeboy's performance until he got his rocks off. Once he was done, the next dopeboy violated her until he came, and so did the next one and the next one and the next one after that. While the last one was busy blowing Martha's back out, one of his homeboys took interest in her jacket. He stole a second look at the action, then rummaged through her jacket's pockets until he came up with her STD test results. His eyes bucked and he smacked his hand over his opened mouth. He tapped one of the other dopeboys on his shoulder. He turned around with an annoyed look on his face having had his entertainment interrupted. He snatched the STD test results and read them over. He was just as shocked by the discovery as the last nigga. Martha had tested positive for HIV, herpes, syphilis and gonorrhea. She contracted all of these diseases during her time inside of the shooting gallery where Ramone had found her.

"Yo, Supreme, that bitch livin' foul! Ol' girl got HIV, herpes, syphilis, the whole nine," the dope boy shouted across the basement, waving the test results at the dope boy currently sexing Martha.

With that announcement, the dope boy that was currently putting it to Martha snatched his dick out of her. He ran over to the other dope boy while pulling up his jeans and zipping them up. He snatched the STD test results away from him and read over them.

"Awwww, fuck, son! This fuckin' bitch is tainted!" the dope boy who'd snatched the test results informed the others.

"Fuck with me, you know I got it! Hahahahahahahahaha!" Martha laughed like a fucking maniac, throat rolling up and down her neck. "You boys know what they say, right? All pussy ain't good pussy! Hahahahahahahahaha!" She threw her head back laughing even harder than she did the first time.

"Bitch, shut the fuck up!" The dope boy ran over and punched her dead in her mouth. She spat blood on the carpet, then looked back up at him. Lowering her gaze, she smiled devilishly at him, displaying her blood-stained teeth. Her maniacal laughing started low and gradually grew. It was driving the dope boy crazy. Holding his hands over his ears, he balled up his face and paced the floor, trying to block out her taunting laughter. "Shut up, bitch! Shut up, shut up, shut up!"

"Yo, man, you—you can get rid of this shit, right? We can't—we can't die from herpes!" one of the dope boys said, looking over the STD results again.

"Herpes stays wit'chu, bro. And HIV will eventually kill you." another dope boy told him.

"Hahahahahahahahahahaha! You see what'cha get?" Martha looked around at all of the faces of the dope boys. "You see what'chu get runnin' around wit'cho li'l hot asses tryna fuck everything that has holes? Hahahahahahahahahahaha!"

"Shut up! Shut the fuck up!" The dope boy Martha had been taunting stopped pacing the floor and upped his pole on her. She wasn't afraid of dying any more. She looked him straight in his eyes, smiling devilishly again. "Laugh again, and I swear on everythang I love I'ma put one in yo' brain, bitch. Go ahead and try me."

After laying down the gauntlet, the dope boy locked eyes with Martha and dared her to challenge him. She could see he was serious about whacking her, but she didn't give a mad-ass fuck. She'd lost nearly everything she loved in life besides Ramone, but she believed she wasn't any good to him alive, so it didn't matter if she was dead.

"Ha...ha...ha," Martha said slowly.

The dope boy scowled and pulled the trigger.

Bocka!

Chapter 20

Blood and brain fragments splattered against Martha's face and titties. The dope boy fired his gun by the side of her face as he fell lifelessly to the floor. As soon as he hit the carpet, Shakur The God and the other dope boys upped their guns. They turned around and sent slugs at Toya and the old dope fiend who were sending heat at them from the staircase. Shakur The God and the dope boys had pistols while Toya and the old dopefiend had some fully loaded automatic shit. One by one, the dope boys met their deaths as bullets melted their faces and tattooed bodies.

"Aaaahhhh!"

"Gahhhhhh!"

"Raaaahhhh!"

The dope boys collapsed where they were firing their guns from and bled out onto the carpet. Shakur The God caught one in his shoulder and in his lower abs. Bleeding profusely, he ducked and dodged the bullets flying every which way, trying to reach Martha. Tucking his banger in his waistband, he took the gold necklace from around his neck that held the gold skeleton key that could open the shackles around her wrists and ankles. He ignored the screams, gunfire, and the smell of gunpowder as he went about the task of unlocking all of the shackles. He threw Martha in a headlock from behind. She gritted and tried to pry his arm from around her neck, to no avail. When the last of the dope boys fell, Toya and the old dopefiend took the time to reload their automatic weapons. Seeing his window of opportunity quickly closing, Shakur The God placed his gun to the side of Martha's head and made his way over to the bar. Toya and the old dopefiend upped their fully loaded automatics to blow those dreadlocks off his skull, but seeing he had Martha at his mercy, they stayed their hands.

"That's right, bitch and bitch-nigga, slow y'all's muthafucka rolls 'fore I drop this old whore right here. Matter of fact, fuck that, y'all toss them shits," Shakur The God demanded of them with his upper lip peeled back in a sneer. His menacing eyes shifted from

Toya to the old dopefiend. If they made any sudden moves, then it was all over for Martha's dopehead ass.

The old dopefiend, still pointing his pole at Shakur The God, looked at Toya to see how she wanted to handle the situation. She gave him a nod. He dropped his gun. She released hers after he did. It was midway to the floor when she swiftly upped a pistol with both hands and squeezed the trigger, blowing off his left ear. He yelped as he let go of Martha and fell to the floor, dropping his gun. Down on his hands and knees, Shakur The God crawled behind the bar and pulled down a lever.

Toya made her way down the staircase with her gun leading the way. She made her way around the bar cautiously, knowing she was going to finish Shakur's old hoe ass once and for all. She got the surprise of a lifetime when he wasn't behind the bar. A surprised look came over her face. It was like he had vanished without a trace.

"You...you look so...so familiar," Martha told the old dope-fiend, touching the side of his face after he'd picked up the automatic weapon he'd dropped. "Where do I know you from?" she asked, looking deep into his eyes.

"That's a story for another time," the old dopefiend told her, passing her panties and jeans to her. "Right now we needa focus on getting the hell up outta here before Jake shows up."

"Where is my baby, Toya?" Martha asked her while slipping into her panties and then stepping into her jeans one leg at a time.

"He's outside," Toya said, tucking her gun at the small of her back and approaching her. She slipped out of her jacket and passed it to Martha.

"What happened to homeboy?" the old dopefiend asked with a frown, referring to Shakur The God.

"I don't know," Toya shrugged her shoulders. "He slipped outta here somehow. Must be a trapdoor or some shit behind that fuckin' bar."

"Come on. Maybe we can catch up with 'em," the old dopefiend replied, hurrying up the staircase.

Toya watched as Martha limped to the opposite side of the basement and picked up a slip of paper. She could see feces and blood had saturated the ass of her jeans. She cringed, thinking of the pain she was in after having been brutally raped by all of those savage-ass dope boys. She walked over to her, locking her arm around hers. Together, they made their way towards the staircase slowly so as not to cause Martha any more pain.

"We've gotta get chu to a hospital, ma," Toya told her.

"I'll be, unh, okay. I just needa wash up," Martha told her.

The lever Shakur The God pulled down caused the bar to slide back and reveal a passage that led out into the gangway. Shakur The God kicked out the trapdoor and crawled his way out to freedom. Holding the gunshot wound he sustained to his lower abs, he looked up and down the gangway, making sure there wasn't anyone around that wanted him dead. When he thought the coast was clear, he slowly made his way down the narrow gangway, leaving smears of blood on the side of the brownstone.

Arrrr, fuck, this shit hurt. And a nigga starting to feel dizzy from losin' so much blood, God, Shakur The God thought as he inched his way to the end of the brownstone. He had a violet and black Ducati Super Sport parked in the backyard. Though his keys to the motorcycle were inside of his crib, he had an extra one that he kept underneath the mat in front of the back door. Once he got his hands on those keys, he could make his way out of the danger zone and to the nearest hospital.

Shakur The God tensed, seeing a dark figure run to the end of the gangway. He was wounded and without a strap, so he was at whomever it was mercy.

"Yo,' God, you good? I heard mad shots comin' from yo' spot so I came running over," the dark figure told him.

"Aye, yo', Lahkim, that you?" Shakur The God asked, squinting his eyes trying to get a good look at him.

"Yeah, it's me, G. Come on. I've gotta get chu the fuck outta here," Lahkim replied. He tucked his gun and outstretched his hand.

Shakur The God grasped his hand with his bloody one. Lahkim pulled him out of the gangway and into him, smiling deceptively. Shakur The God's eyes bucked and his mouth quivered. It wasn't Lahkim he'd been talking to this entire time. It was Ramone!

Blocka, blocka, blocka!

The gangway exploded with light each time Ramone fired his gun into Shakur The God's belly. He staggered backwards, holding his stomach with both hands, staring up at Ramone accusingly. He turned around in an attempt to run, but winded up falling to the ground. Blood spilling over his chin, he began his crawl towards the opposite end of the gangway, where salvation awaited.

Ramone casually walked up behind him with the warm gun in his hand and pressed his sneaker against his back. "My pops once told me one day you'll be spending your last day with someone and you won't know it. I call bullshit on that though. 'Cause I *know* this will most definitely be my last day with the likes of you."

Blocka, blocka, blocka, blocka!

Four head shots to the back of Shakur The God's dreads guaranteed he wouldn't be waking up in the morning. Ramone tucked his gun at the small of his back and looked down the gangway. He saw Toya, Martha, and the old dopefiend hauling ass across the street toward his whip. He took off running down the gangway after them.

***

Ramone zipped up the street and debris flew up in the air. He looked into the side view mirror to see if anyone was following him, but he didn't see a soul. He adjusted the rearview mirror and looked up at it. He frowned, seeing Martha hugged up with the old dopefiend. He reasoned that since they had the same lifestyle that it was likely that they knew each other from the streets. Ramone wanted to ask his mother what happened back at the brownstone, but seeing the relaxed look on her face changed his mind. He looked to Toya, who was staring out of the passenger window and asked her in a hushed tone.

Toya took a breath before giving him the rundown. Ramone's eyes became watery listening to her relay everything that transpired back at Shakur's spot. Tears broke down his cheeks. He quickly wiped them away, but the next bomb she dropped on him opened up the floodgates.

"Baby, there's something else," Toya told him, reaching inside of her jacket's pocket.

"Something else like what?" Ramone's forehead wrinkled with wonder.

Toya passed Ramone a wrinkled, folded slip of paper. He kept an eye on the road ahead as he unfolded the paper and read over it. The news of his mother's sexual transmitted diseases was devastating to him. He felt like his heart had been ripped out of his chest. He found it hard to breathe. Toya's eyes became consumed with worry. She interlocked her fingers with Ramone's and rubbed his back to comfort him.

"Breathe, baby...breathe...nice and easy...nice and easy," Toya spoke with the voice of an angel in an attempt to calm her man. Ramone took her advice, breathing slow and easily. He began to wind down, and became calm. He drove up to a red traffic light, sniffling and wiping his eyes with the back of his hand.

"I love you." Toya told him.

Ramone looked at her. "I love you too."

Ramone kissed her and looked back up at the rearview mirror. He saw his mother nestled against the old dopefiend, snoring softly.

Damn, Momma, goddamn, Ramone thought with fresh tears brewing in his eyes. *I lost bruh, and now I'm gonna lose you. I don't know how much my heart can take.*

***

Ramone drove back to Toya's crib, where she busied herself bathing Martha in a nice hot bath of Epsom salts. Ramone and the old dopefiend kicked it in the living room. The old dopefiend talked while Ramone half listened. His thoughts were consumed by his mother's current state and how much time he'd have with her before she was gone—like everyone else he loved.

"Say, youngsta, youngsta!"

Ramone's head snapped up and he blinked his eyes repeatedly. He ran his hand down his face and looked at the old dopefiend who'd been calling him. "What up, yo?"

"It's been one hell of a night, kid. Do you mind? You know," the old dopefiend pretended to shoot himself with dope. Ramone thought on it for a second before giving him the nod to go ahead and get high.

"My man." The old dopefiend tapped his fist against his chest. He snatched off his beanie and winced while slipping his hoodie over his head. He was now in a dingy wife beater and over-sized black denim jeans. He removed a velvet pouch attached to his waistband containing all of his paraphernalia and set everything out on the coffee table.

The old dopefiend finished preparing the heroin. He dropped a piece of cotton in the spoon to absorb the dope in its liquid form. Once the drug had cooled a little, he tied a tourniquet around his arm and pulled it tight with his teeth. He licked his lips as he drew the heroin into his syringe, made sure there weren't any air bubbles in it, and stuck the needle into the pronounced vein in his forearm.

Ramone had been watching the old dopefiend the entire time he'd been preparing his fix. He knew it would be a matter of time before the drug worked its magic on him, so he had to inquire about him and his mother's relationship. Ramone made an ugly face after swallowing what was left of his drink. He plopped down on the couch beside the old dopefiend when he began to push down on the plunger of the syringe.

"Say, bruh, I've been meaning to thank you for hitting me up when you seen Madukes was in trouble," Ramone told him. He then took out a small bankroll of twenty-dollar bills from the small pocket of his jeans and placed it on the coffee table. "Thanks a li'l token of my appreciation."

The old dopefiend's eyes fluttered and his lips formed a one-sided smile. He leaned back against the couch, biting down on his bottom lip and pulling the syringe from out of his arm.

"Th—thanks."

Chapter 21

Ramone heard movement at his back, so he glanced over his shoulder. Toya was escorting his mother out of the bathroom and heading down the hallway. He focused his attention back on the old dopefiend. He could tell by the blissful look across his face that he was on cloud 9 and wouldn't be coming down any time soon. Still, he had to press him for the information he wanted. It was killing him not knowing how he and his mother had known each other.

"Look, I'm not the type of nigga to beat around the bush, so I'ma just come out with it." Ramone adjusted himself on the couch to get comfortable. "I saw you and my moms hugged up in the backseat whispering and shit. I take it you two know each other. What I'm tryna figure out is from where?"

The old dopefiend was ten miles down the road in Lala Land. It was as if Ramone wasn't even sitting there beside him. It wasn't until he snapped his fingers in front of his face and shouted at him that he awoke with a start. He looked around like he'd been spun around in a circle until he was dizzy. He locked eyes with Ramone, sat the syringe down and settled back on the couch.

"My bad, young'un, but this Rebirth shit is the best dope I done had in quite some time," the old dopefiend assured him. "Now what was it that you wanted?"

"How do you and my moms know each other?"

"Oh, uh, you mean Martha?" He began to doze off again, but shook it off. "Me and, uh, me and Martha go way, way back."

"How far back? Y'all used to be an item or something back in the day?"

The old dopefiend bowed his head. Frustrated, Ramone scowled and pimp slapped his ass. His head snapped up and he held his stinging red cheek. He didn't know what the fuck was going on, but the look on Ramone's face told him he better not nod off again. The young nigga looked like he meant business, especially with that gun in his hand.

"Say, OG, wake yo' ass up. I gotta few questions that need to be answered, ASAP."

The old dopefiend was hot at first. He started to bust Ramone in his mouth for putting his dick beater on him, but he decided to let his rage subside and entertain his little game of twenty-one questions. The old dopefiend cleared his throat and sat up in his seat, wincing. "I know yo' mother from way back in the day. We used to be a thang. We had some good times, some really good times."

"My nigga, that's my Madukes, so tread lightly. Nah'mean?"

The dopefiend looked at him with sleepy eyes. "Relax, young'un. You asked for the rundown and the only way I know how to give it to you is raw and uncut. Ya dig?"

"I don't give a fuck! My warning still stands." Ramone mad dogged him. "If you don't like it, then we can reenact that scene you and my shorty made back at Shakur's." The old dopefiend laughed and grimaced in pain. "The fuck is so funny?"

"I told yo' mother outta you and Jayshawn, you'd be the feisty one," the old dopefiend replied. "Neither one of y'all would take anyone's shit, but you were always the one ready to go to war. It didn't matter who it was. How big they were. Or who they had backing 'em."

"Man, I'm sicka playing games with yo' ass," Ramone said through clenched teeth. He grabbed the old dopefiend by his neck and pressed his tool against his cheek. "Now who the hell are you to my moms?"

For the first time, Ramone noticed the old dopefiend was pale and sweating like he'd run a full-court of basketball. He found this odd, but chose to ignore it. Right now, he was only concerned with finding out who he was.

"Take a wild guess," the old dopefiend told him, staring into his eyes.

Ramone's eyes bugged. His mouth fell open. He took his gun from homeboy's cheek and sat back on the couch. He then looked at old boy again. He imagined him clean-shaven and about twenty years younger. "Well, I'll be damned. Chico?" Ramone uttered his name like he wasn't for sure it was him.

"Yeah. Your dear ol' dad. Arrrrrrgh!" Chico's face balled up in excruciation. He appeared to be sweating more now.

Ramone seemed to be concerned with his condition now. "What's up?"

"Back at the—at the—brown—st—stone—I caught a couple." The old dopefiend touched the side of his wife beater and his fingertips came away bloody.

Setting his gun down on the coffee table, Ramone lifted up his wife beater and examined his wounds. He was bleeding like a stuck pig hanging upside down from a meat hook.

"Man, this shit looks bad. I mean real bad," Ramone said to no one in particular. He then looked up at his father. "Yo, son, why the fuck didn't you say something, huh? We coulda gotten you to a hospital or something."

"No—no hospitals—the police will come—come around asking questions," Chico assured him, wincing. Sweat dripped from the corner of his brow. "Then they'll put two and two together and connect—connect us back to all of those murders back at the brownstone."

"Toya!" Ramone called out to her from over his shoulder.

Toya, clutching her gun with both hands, crept inside of the living room. She surveyed her surroundings, ready to eliminate any threats. When she didn't see any, she relaxed and walked around the couch. As soon as she saw how Chico was bleeding, she knew why Ramone was calling for her.

"What happened?" Toya asked, tucking her gun at the small of her back.

"Back at Shakur's. He was hit," Ramone replied in a panic.

"Check and see if the slugs are still in 'em. I'll go get the first-aid kit." Toya ran down the hallway, bumping past Martha. She'd changed into a fresh set of Toya's clothes and sneakers. When she saw Chico was wounded, she ran around the couch and kneeled at his side.

"What happened to 'em?" Martha asked with a frown.

Ramone told his mother what happened to Chico as he leaned him forward. When he lifted his wife beater, there were two gunshot wounds leaking crazily.

"Fuck, fuck, fuck!" Ramone cussed like a sailor, leaning Chico back gently.

"Is he gonna be awright?" Martha asked, holding Chico's bloody hand with both of hers.

"No. This is—this is i—it," Chico told her. Instantly, her cheeks flooded.

"What's the deal?" Toya asked, returning to the living room with a yellow first-aid kit.

"He's—he's bleeding like hell, babe," Ramone told her, looking fearful.

Ramone felt his eyes begin to water. He was scared of losing his father, and it surprised him. For years, he'd promised himself if he laid eyes on him again, he'd beat him to a bloody pulp. But all that had changed in this moment. He didn't want to lose his old man. He had a million and one questions he wanted to ask him. If he should perish, then the answers to those very questions would perish along with him. Ramone was beginning to believe he was cursed. It was like everyone he came into contact with ended up dead.

"Ma, I'ma need you to apply pressure to his wounds to try to slow the bleeding," Toya told Martha as she pulled a pair of latex gloves over her hands and flexed her fingers inside of them.

Martha did as she was told. Chico took two pictures out of his back pocket and passed them to Ramone. The first one was of Jayshawn, Ramone, Chico, and Martha dressed in their Sunday best. The second was of a young Chico, a tall, brolic, African man who looked like he'd been carved out of a hunk of chocolate, and a beautiful brown-skinned woman with slanted-eyes, high cheekbones and full-lips. They were all dressed in traditional garments from their native land. Ramone gathered that this must have been his father's parents and his grandparents.

"They're—they're your grand—grandparents, son," Chico told him. "Your—your grandfather was once the chief enforcer for a—a very prominent figure in—in Nigeria."

"Who?"

"A—a man by the name of K—King U—Uche. Grrrrr." Chico growled in agony as Toya leaned him forward to dress his gunshot wounds. "Mar—Martha, I'm sorry. I'm so, so sorry for all the wrong I caused you and my boys. My helping to save your life was the least I could do to try to repay—"

He was suddenly hushed by Martha placing her finger against his lips. "All is forgiven. You hear me? All is forgiven," Martha assured him. "You just pull your ass outta this fire so we can be a family again. You hear?" Chico nodded. She cupped his face and kissed him tenderly.

"What about you, son? You—you think you can find it in—in yo' heart to forgive your old man?"

Ramone looked at his mother. She nodded for him to say yes, but before he could, he was interrupted by someone ringing the doorbell.

"Who the hell could that be?" Toya looked up from what she was doing.

"It's probably Jabari. He hit me up on the way over here," Ramone informed her.

Toya went back to tending to Chico's wounds while Ramone answered the door. He peeked through the blinds to see Jabari standing at the front door. His clothes were disheveled and his face looked like he'd spent the day sparring with Apollo Creed.

"Is that him, babe?" Toya called out.

"Yeah. It's this nigga," Ramone replied, switching hands with his gun and unlocking the front door. As soon as he opened the front door, he stood aside to allow Jabari passage.

He shuffled in over the threshold tucking his tool at the front of his jeans. While Ramone was locking the door behind Jabari, he was peeking through the blinds to make sure he hadn't been followed. His eyes widened when he thought he saw movement in the backseat of the truck he'd driven there. He squeezed his eyes shut and popped them back open. He examined the SUV again and reasoned he was seeing things.

"My nigga, you look like shit," Ramone said after inspecting Jabari. "What the fuck happened to you?"

"Mannnnn, it's been one hell of a night for the kid. I don't even know where to begin." Jabari made his way towards the kitchen.

"Yo, y'all got something to drink up in this piece, God? A nigga parched as a motha."

"There's some of everything you can name in the fridge. Help yourself." Toya told him. She was now working on the front of Chico's wounds.

"Thanks," Jabari replied, taking in Chico and Martha's appearance. "I see y'all been to hell and back too, son."

"Yeah. We've all hadda night to remember." Ramone stated. "I'll fill you in on ours, but I wanna hear what's up wit'chu first."

Jabari popped the lid on a bottle of Heineken and tossed the cap inside the waste basket. He made his way out of the kitchen as he began telling Ramone about his night.

"...Next thing I know, mad African niggas kick in the door."

"Oh, yeah? Who were they?" Ramone inquired.

"Who you think, Slime? They were Sanka's boys." Jabari took a swig of beer. He frowned when he finally noticed who the man was on the couch. "Yo, ain't that the fiend that we—"

Jabari was cut short by the ringing of Ramone's cell phone.

Chapter 22

Ramone's face balled up, wondering who it was hitting him up since the call was "Private". He started to ignore it, but his curiosity got the best of him and he decided to open it. He answered the call and watched Jabari walk past him. He approached the couch, taking a closer look at Chico.

"Who this?" Ramone asked.

"Yo, son, it's me. Don't hang up!"

"Paperchase?"

When Jabari heard his right-hand man's name, he looked back at Ramone and took another swig of his beer. He was watching him closely now.

I thought Scorpion said that dick sucka was dead, Jabari thought. *That's another soft-ass nigga. Shit must be hereditary.*

"Yeah, it's me."

"What's the deal?"

Ramone paced the floor, feeling Jabari's eyes on him the entire time. The mood in the room shifted and the tension in the air became so thick it was suffocating.

"That nigga Jabari there?"

"Yeah, why?" Ramone stopped pacing and looked up at Jabari. He held his gaze as he listened to what Paperchase had to say.

"He killed yo' brother, Blood! He killed Jayshawn."

Jabari watched Ramone's face twist into a mask of hatred. Instantly, he knew he'd been informed that he was the one that had taken out his brother. Ramone dropped his cell phone and reached for his gun. Jabari launched his Heineken bottle at him. Ramone moved aside and the bottle flew past his head. Ramone upped his pole but by then, Jabari had pulled Martha into him and placed his gun into the side of her head. Holding his arm, she looked around, afraid for her life.

"Fuck is up, Ramone?" Toya asked. She'd pulled her tool when Jabari snatched up Martha. Both of her hands were wrapped around her gun which was pinned on him.

"This nigga killed my brother!" Ramone broke the news.

143

"Yep. Sho' in the fuck did, and I'ma push ya mom's shit back, if y'all don't drop them fucking guns," Jabari threatened, cocking the hammer on his gun and slowly walking back towards the front door.

"Why'd you kill my brother?" Ramone asked, slowly moving in on Jabari.

"Nigga popped shit at me like he was some great, big ol' steppa, so I laid his bitch-ass down," Jabari confessed. "Plus, I figured if I convinced you Paperchase did it, you'd see to it that he was dead. Thus, leaving me with only two more niggas to smoke to secure the plug on the Rebirth."

"Son, you're one slimy, lowdown muthafucka," Ramone told him. Tears burst through his eyes and his nostrils flared. He turned red in the face and a vein twitched at his temple.

"Back up! You back the fuck up right now!" Jabari shouted, pointing his gun at Ramone and stopping him cold in his tracks. He then swayed his pistol over to Toya and back over to Ramone. This entire time, Martha was shedding tears with a faraway look in her eyes. She was thinking of how brutally her oldest son was murdered. She had flashbacks of seeing him laid up in the morgue, a pale blue complexion with his throat slit. Her bottom lips quivered and she clutched Jabari's arm tighter.

"He killed my baby...you killed my baby...you bastard!" Martha shouted before sinking her teeth into Jabari's forearm, growling. She shook her head from side to side like a wild-ass pitbull.

"Aaaaaaaah!" Jabari threw his head back screaming, blood pouring out of his forearm. He whacked Martha upside the head and kicked her to the floor. Cradling his wounded arm, he retreated to the front door with bullets flying around him. He'd made it out of the house by the time Ramone and Toya kneeled down to his mother.

"Ma, you good?" Ramone inquired.

"I'll be fine, baby boy." Martha winced, rubbing the back of her head. She could already feel a lump forming on it.

Upon hearing her man's mother was okay; Toya jumped up and ran out of the house behind Jabari. Ramone hugged his mother to him, kissed the top of her head, and ran out of the front door after Toya.

Toya and Ramone made it outside in time to see Jabari driving off in his truck. They sent a few bullets at him, but only managed to scratch the bulletproof SUV. Running to a stop in the middle of the residential block, the couple dumped on the vehicle as it grew smaller and smaller down the road.

"Fuck!" Toya cussed, hating they weren't able to stop Jabari's scandalous ass. She lowered her smoking pole beside Ramone.

"We've gotta stash these guns. I know Jake is coming." Ramone grabbed Toya's hand and led her back towards the house.

Ramone and Toya returned to the house to find Martha at Chico's side. Her head was bowed and she was holding his hand. Her shoulders rocked as she cried her eyes out.

"Ma, what's the matter?" Ramone asked.

Martha lifted her head and wiped her eyes. "He's...he's dead, baby. Your father's dead."

Ramone looked at Chico. His eyes were wide open staring at nothing while his mouth was hanging open. Taking a deep breath, Ramone dropped his head and massaged the bridge of his nose. Toya took his gun away from him, hugged him, and kissed him on his temple. She rubbed his back for a second before walking away to hide the guns.

Ramone walked over to Chico. He stared down at him for a moment before sweeping his eyes closed. "Yeah, I forgive you, Pops." He answered the question his old man posed to him earlier that night. He then picked up his cell phone where he'd dropped it and dialed 9-1-1. As he gave the dispatcher the story he'd formulated in his brain, Toya hugged him from behind and laid the side of her face against his back.

***

Jabari jumped in behind the wheel of the bulletproof truck and sped away. Glancing over his shoulder, he saw Ramone and Toya running out of the house. They stopped halfway out of the yard and opened fire on the stolen truck.

The bullets ricocheted off the black armored SUV and left scratches behind. Ramone and Toya ran out into the street and started blasting at the back of the truck. They fired on it until it was out of range. Jabari looked up into the rearview mirror and they were running back to the house. His heart nearly leaped out of his chest when a masked man lifted his head up in the backseat and blocked his view of him. Jabari went to grab his gun off the passenger seat when he felt a pinch at the side of his neck. He felt light-headed and drowsy. His vision became cloudy. He grabbed hold of the steering wheel to keep from crashing, but he couldn't see where he was going. He narrowed his eyes into slits and leaned forward the windshield.

The masked man saw that they were speeding towards an intersection where cars were whipping back and forth. His eyes bugged and he dove to the floor of the backseat. Jabari fell asleep behind the wheel and the truck went off course. It crashed into a row of cars lined up on the right side of the residential block before eventually smashing into the back of a Toyota pickup truck. Instantly, the air-bag deployed in Jabari's face and the security alarm blared.

"Uuuuuh." The masked man rose from off the floor of the back seat. He rubbed his head and looked around. Leaning up front, he checked the pulse in Jabari's neck to make sure he was alive. He then called his accomplice through his watch so he could pull the van up. As soon as the masked man hopped out of the SUV, the van drove up alongside him and a second masked man slid the side door open. He tossed the first masked man handcuffs to cuff up Jabari. Holding a black pillowcase, he jumped down onto the street upon broken glass from the collision. Once his partner had Jabari's wrists restrained behind his back, he slipped the black pillowcase over his head and helped his accomplice load him into the back of the van.

***

New York City's Finest was first on the scene. Then the coroners showed up. They loaded Chico's body into the back of their vehicle and whisked him away. Ramone and Toya were being questioned by one of four police officers. He scribbled what he was being told on a small tablet while he stood beside his partner. A third cop was using the bathroom. The fourth and final one was busy looking at family portraits on the wall. While all of this was going on, Martha was inside the kitchen, placing donuts and cups of coffee upon a tray. She made her way around the living room allowing the cops to grab a cup of coffee and a donut of their choosing. The cops either nodded their appreciation for their tasty treat or flat out thanked her.

Ramone looked at the name tags of every cop inside the living room. His forehead wrinkled when he noticed their last names were traditionally American. He thought this shit was strange since they had the classic African features and occasionally spoke with a third world country accent. It was almost as if they were trying to disguise their natural voices.

Ramone took in the appearances of the cops as they indulged in their coffee and donuts. He glanced in each of their directions to find them staring at him over their cups as they took sips from them. Johnson, Wangler, Aubert, Spencer. He read their name tags again and looked back up into their faces. They were all watching him as if they were waiting for him to make a move.

"These muthafuckas aren't cops!" Ramone took a step back and reached for the gun in his waistband. A look of confusion crossed his face when he came up empty-handed. That's when he realized he'd given his piece to Toya to hide. *Shit!*

The cops, who were actually Sanka's hitters, dropped their cups of coffee and snatched their guns from their black leather holsters. They were almost in sync when they pointed their pistols at Ramone, Toya, and Martha. They threw their hands up in the air and looked around the living room. Those fake-ass cops were mad dogging them and anxiously awaiting to exercise their trigger-fingers.

"Down on ya knees wit ya hands behind ya head!" one of the Nigerians demanded in his thick accent. "Now cross your legs! If anyone of yew tries anythin', I swear to Gawd I'll shoot yew in dee face, I promise."

The three Nigerians kept their guns pinned on Ramone and them. A moment later, the fourth Nigerian cop emerged from the hallway, drawing a sedative from a small bottle with his syringe. He walked down the row that Ramone, Toya and Martha formed, injecting them with the substance. One after the other, they became lightheaded and fell down onto the carpet. As soon as they were out, the rest of the Nigerians holstered their weapons and went about the task of handcuffing them. They then pulled black pillowcases over their heads and proceeded to load them into the back of a police van. Once the last of their cargo was on board and accounted for, one of the last two Nigerians left on the scene pounded on the back of the police van and it drove away. He then pulled out his cell phone and hit up Sanka. He answered as he hopped in behind the wheel and slammed the door shut behind him.

"Tell me something good," Sanka came on the line.

"We have dem, boss," the Nigerian replied.

"You remember how to get here?"

"Yes. See you soon." The Nigerian disconnected the call. He cranked up the car, backed up, and took off down the block.

Chapter 23

Paperchase hurried up the steps of his crib with his cell phone glued to his ear. He closed and locked the front door behind him before marching to his bedroom. As soon as Ramone picked up his call, he dropped a bomb on him: Jabari was the nigga that rocked Jayshawn to sleep. Paperchase could hear Ramone and Jabari in a heated argument. Then came the deafening gunshots that made him frown and snatched his ear away from the phone.

"Ramone! Ramone! Shiiit!" Paperchase disconnected the call and put his cellular in his pocket. He grabbed an old Nike gym bag out of the closet, grabbed a butcher's knife out of the kitchen, and returned to his bedroom. He stripped the mattress bare and slit open the sewn area on the side of it. Bankrolls of drug money spilled out onto the floor almost instantly. By the time he finished stuffing his gym bag, it looked like it was going to burst at the seams.

Paperchase recovered a gun case from the top shelf of his closet. He removed a .45 automatic from the case, chambered a hollow tip round into its head, and then tucked it at the front of his waistband. He stuffed two fully-loaded magazines into his pocket, slipped the gym bag's strap over his shoulders and walked out of his bedroom. He opened the front door and gave his spot one last look before heading out of the door.

Paperchase slammed the door to his brother's whip and cranked it up. He didn't know exactly where he was headed, but he was sure he'd make up his mind once he'd gotten on the highway. Paperchase was just about to put his car into drive when a man as dark as the night popped up in the backseat. He pulled a black pillowcase over his face and he thrashed around in the driver seat. His struggle to get free was useless. The assailant was stronger than him and had a hold like a king crab.

Paperchase grabbed his gun from his waistband and held it awkwardly over his shoulder. He squeezed its trigger twice, but the assailant moved his head aside. The bullets punched holes into the ceiling of the vehicle. When he went to fire the pistol again, the assailant smacked it out of his hand and brandished a syringe. Using his teeth, he snatched the cap off the syringe and spat it out. He feasted his eyes on a thick, juicy vein alongside Paperchase's neck and then jabbed it with the needle. He pressed down on the plunger and the sedative surged through the needle. The drug flowed through Paperchase's bloodstream. Its effects caused him to move slower and slower until he stopped moving altogether.

The assailant held Paperchase a while longer before releasing the black pillowcase. He checked his wrist watch for the time and then hit someone up. They answered on the first ring.

"I've got 'em," he told whomever in his thick Nigerian accent.

A moment later, a big white van screeched to a halt behind him alongside the curb. The assailant looked over his shoulder in time to see the side door of the vehicle sliding open. His acquaintance stuck his masked face out of the door. He looked up and down the street for anyone that may have been watching them. When he didn't see a soul, he jumped out of the van and hurried up Paperchase's driveway. He handcuffed Paperchase's wrists behind his back and then assisted his partner in loading him inside of the van.

***

Hakim walked around the hostages, yanking the black pillowcases off their heads one by one, revealing their identities. There was Ramone, Jabari, Paperchase, Scorpion, Toya, and Martha. They all frowned under the lighting in the living room. They'd been in the darkness for so long the light felt like needles to their eyes. Ramone, Jabari, Paperchase, Scorpion, Toya, and Martha looked around the living room as the stinging sensation in their eyes began to wear off. They were all shocked to see each other in one room and more so that others who were thought dead were actually alive.

They took in the rest of the inhabitants of the living room. They were surrounded by African hitters—including Abdullah and Hakim. Among them was the man that had orchestrated everything that had transpired thus far. Usually he wore the garments that represented his culture, but he'd traded those in for something more casual. He stood before them wearing a royal blue Nike dad hat and matching Nike tracksuit. A gold cable link chain hung loosely around his neck. It was attached to a saucer-sized diamond studded medallion with the continent of Africa at the center of it.

"There's those of you who don't know who the hell I am. Then there's those of you who're asking yourselves, 'who in the fuck is this guy?' " Sanka said, pacing the floor with his head down, holding his hands behind him.

Keeping his eyes on Sanka, Martin spoke to Olivia in a hushed tone. "I take it this is that wealthy African prick that's after you."

Olivia, whose eyes stayed on Sanka too, replied back to him. "Yeah. That's that dickhead," she confirmed, spitting on the floor.

"Well, for those of you that do know who I am, why don't one of you fill the others in on the deal we made," Sanka said, still pacing the floor with his hands held behind his back.

Paperchase looked around at everyone. No one looked like they were going to say anything. He thought it was best he spoke up so he could see exactly what Sanka had in store for them. Paperchase cleared his throat and spoke loud and clear so everyone in attendance could hear him. All eyes were on him as he went on to tell how he'd been abducted by Sanka and the deal they'd made for him to be the sole distributor of Rebirth.

"Good, now tell them the other details of the deal," Sanka urged. He'd stopped pacing the floor and was standing beside Hakim. His eyes were focused on Paperchase as he sharpened a shiny black metal machete with a small Nigerian flag hanging from the bottom of its handle.

Olivia's eyes bugged and she swallowed the ball of nervousness in her throat. She knew any minute then someone was going to die in that room, if not all of them.

"The deal was for me to take out three men of his choosing," Paperchase continued with what he had to say. "I don't know who two of those dudes are, but one of them was my best friend and brother—Jabari." He hung his head in shame after uttering his lifelong comrade's name. He'd always considered himself a real nigga but he'd lost that title due to his greed and selfishness.

"Now you." Sanka pointed his machete at Olivia, then at Scorpion. "Then you." He pointed the machete at Jabari. "And finally, your punk ass," he said with hateful eyes and a curled top lip. He was hot about Jabari and his goons robbing his spots and kidnapping his cousin. Although he had it in mind to behead him, he was thinking of other ways to punish him for his violations.

Olivia told her side of the story, Scorpion told him, and then Jabari gave his raw and uncut truth. He even threw out there how he'd murdered Jayshawn to gas Ramone up to kill Paperchase. Hearing this hurtful truth again enraged Ramone, Martha, and Toya. They tried to charge Jabari, but the Africans standing over them, forced them back down on their knees.

Martha bowed her head and started crying. Teardrops fell from her eyes and splashed on the floor. Seeing his mother grieving fucked with Ramone's mind and heart. He hated to see her so vulnerable. He rubbed the side of his face against hers as tears were on the verge of sliding down his own.

"It's okay, ma. I'ma get 'em," Ramone swore. "As soon as I get my chance, I'ma lay his bitch ass down. Word to Jayshawn." He kissed his mother's cheek and rubbed the side of his face against hers again. He then turned to Toya, kissing her and rubbing the side of his face against hers as well.

Jibbs and Sankeesy stood among the cluster of African hitters in the living room. Holding hands, they listened closely to everyone detailing the particulars of the deal they'd made with Sanka. Each man and woman was more scandalous than the next. All they could do was shake their heads and promise to vet the people in their lives better in the future.

Maniacal laughter drew everyone's attention to Jabari. He was laughing so hard he was crying. Nearly everyone frowned ,wondering what the fuck was so funny. They whispered among each other saying, he'd snapped and gone mad.

"I can't, I can't with y'all niggas, son," Jabari managed to say between laughter. "I get looked at as the bad guy here, but it turns out every last one of you bitches are equally as big a piece of shit as me." He continued his maniacal laughter. "Muthafuckas sold each other out over blow, money, and power. Didn't care who had to get crushed in order to get it either. On gang. You can't trust anybody these days."

Martin stared at Olivia like he didn't know who she was after hearing some of the things she'd done to gain access to Sanka's dope. The entire time he believed she was just some sweet, innocent woman who'd gotten tangled up with the wrong man. That definitely wasn't the case. Little mama was a wolf in sheep's clothing.

Out of the corner of her eye, Olivia could feel Martin's eyes on her. Her face scrunched up and she snapped her head around to him. "What?"

"Nothing. Nothing at all," Martin said, looking somewhere else. *I stick my neck out for this broad, and she turns out to be a bigger piece of shit than most of these guys.*

"I know what you're thinking, and I don't care," Olivia replied. She could tell by the look on Martin's face the way he felt about her had changed. "A bitch hadda do what a bitch hadda do to sit at the top of the food chain, in this male-dominated game."

"Yeah. I hear ya, toots." Martin told her, still looking somewhere else.

"You know what, Martin? All you white muthafuckas are the same," Olivia spat venomously. "You got the nerve to turn yo' nose up at me, when you and your people run an organized crime syndicate where you rob, steal, kill and extort pe—"

Olivia's rant was cut short as something razor sharp sliced through the flesh and bone of her neck. Martin squeezed his eyes into slits as blood splattered against the side of his face. His eyes were opened just enough to see Olivia's severed head fly across the living room. Olivia's head tumbled across the floor and landed before Paperchase. He looked down at the severed head. It was staring at him and he was staring back at it. A shocked expression was on its face. Blood slowly poured from the bottom of it and saturated the floor.

Sankeesy looked away from the terrifying sight. She laid the side of her face against Jibbs' chest and wrapped her arms around him. He kissed the top of her head, rubbed her back, and continued to watch the drama unfold.

"Oh my Lord!" Martha hollered when she saw Olivia's severed head.

Toya closed her eyes and hid her face in the crux of Ramone's neck.

"Lousy, no good, American bitch! That'll teach you to disrespect your king," Sanka said as he stared at Olivia's headless body. It was slumped over beside him and blood was spurting out from where her head used to be. Sanka spat on her corpse. He wiped his machete off on Martin's shoulder, leaned over into his ear and hung his arm around his shoulders. Martin closed his eyes and recited a silent prayer. He knew what was coming next and he wanted to make sure God let him through those pearly gates.

Chapter 24

"Don't tell me you're in your feelings about me dropping this skeezer, huh?" Sanka asked. His lips were so close to Martin's ear he could feel it turning hot and moist.

Martin gave Sanka the evil eye. "Fuck her! You're the asshole I have a beef with."

"Me? What have I done to earn such hostility?" Sanka asked with wrinkled eyebrows. He didn't personally know Martin, so he was curious about the issue he had with him.

"My client died in that explosion you orchestrated back at that bar," Martin told him. "I took that personally, and I aim to collect on that debt."

"I'm sorry about your client. I truly am," Sanka assured him. "But you have to crack open a few eggs if you're gonna make an omelet."

"You bastard!" Martin spat angrily. He attempted to get up, but Sanka held fast.

"Aye, aye, colonizer, calm your pasty, white ass down," Sanka ordered, holding Martin at the back of his collar. "You think you're the only one that's upset here? I had a half a billion dollar pool going on, on who was going to win this little game of mine, but these half-breeds"—he swept his machete around Paperchase, Jabari and Olivia—"Took too long, so I had to give my business partners their funds back and bring this fucking game to an end myself."

"Stop all of your goddamn whining. That shit is over now, fuck-head!" Martin roared angrily at Sanka, sprinkling his face with spit-tle.

Sanka smiled demonically and wiped his face with his sleeve. Standing upright, he cocked his machete back with every intention of chopping off Martin's head.

"You're right. That shit is over now, and so are you!" Sanka grunted as he went to swing the machete into the side of Martin's neck. Martin closed his eyes and tightened his jaws in anticipation of the blade piercing his thick neck.

Ba-Boom!

The doors of the mansion burst open, startling everyone inside of the living room. Everyone looked at the entrance, including Sanka. He had his machete held at mid-swing but was looking in the direction of his unwanted guests. The African hitters who were under his command turned their assault rifles on the intruders.

"Who the fuck are you?" Sanka asked. He squinted his eyes to see who'd barged into the mansion.

"Uncle Uche?" Sankeesy asked, squinting her face.

"Fa—father, you're alive," Sanka said, surprised. The last he'd heard his father had been chopped down by gunfire from an assassin he'd exiled from his kingdom for deliberately disobeying his orders. Though his body hadn't been recovered, Sanka still went ahead and had his funeral.

Upon hearing the rightful king was present, the African hitters under Sanka's command performed like Marines. They stood their assault rifles up on the side of them, stuck their chests out and held their heads up high.

"It is I, my beautiful niece." King Uche spoke from his electric wheelchair which was made to look like a gold throne with purple, suede cushioning.

"But I thought you had been killed," Sankeesy said.

"Nearly. But I was pulled from the brink of death…thanks to the fruit of the Tree of Life," King Uche replied. He pushed the small joystick forward and his chair drove up until he could be seen from head to toe.

King Uche was a heavyset man who stood 6'1" and weighed 266 pounds. He had skin of brass, a shiny bald head, and a full cotton-white beard. He was fitted in a military-green turtleneck and plaid charcoal-gray slacks. His hands were wrapped around the handles of a Thompson submachine gun with a 100-round drum.

Sanka lowered his machete and moved to approach his father. He took three steps before his old man pointed his Tommy gun at him. A look of confusion came across his face. He didn't know what the fuck was going on.

"Daddy, what is the meaning of this? It's me! Your son! Sanka!" Sanka told him with his hand to his chest.

"I know exactly who you are, Demon," King Uche fumed, with his finger outside the trigger guard of his submachine gun. "You ordered my assassination so you could rule over all I brought to fruition. What's worse is you put your cousin, Sankeesy, in danger by having her go along with those numbskull carriers of yours to fetch your precious trap money."

"What? Who would tell you such lies?" Sanka asked. He looked like he was genuinely surprised by his father's claims.

"I have eyes and ears everywhere, boy."

"Eyes," Abdullah stated, stepping forward.

"Ears," Hakim stated lastly, stepping forward.

Sanka's most trusted hands turned out to be spies for his father. They'd been playing him like a fucking fiddle. They had knowledge of King Uche being alive all along.

Right then, the Africans who were under Sanka's command turned their assault rifles on him. Sanka made a 360-degree turn, taking in all the faces of the hitters who wanted his head on a silver platter. He smiled, twisted his hat to the back, and looked at his father.

"Well, old man, it looks like you got me dead to rights. Before you do whatever you have planned for me, I'd like to know one thing." Sanka held up his finger. King Uche nodded for him to continue. "Did you kill the kid?"

King Uche was quiet for a second before he answered, "No. I was able to talk him down before he carried out my murder," he told him. "That boy was young and impressionable. He looked at you like an older brother, which is why you were able to manipulate him in the first place." King Uche became silent for a moment as he thought back to the night the teenager had attempted to kill him. He took out four of his best men before managing to put three into King Uche's chest. If it hadn't been for the fact he had the gift of gab and could talk just about anyone into doing anything, he was sure his ass would have been grass that night.

"Then what did you do with 'em?" Sanka's eyebrows wrinkled curiously.

"He's back home, getting homeschooled and seeing a therapist twice a week," King Uche revealed. "Kid's dealing with a lotta trauma, so he has a mountain of crap he needs to sort out."

The attempt on King Uche's life left him paralyzed from the waist down but in time, with the consumption of the fruit from the Tree of Life, he'd eventually regain the ability to walk again. The shooter was a novice, a thirteen-year-old Nigerian kid named Kunta whom King Uche adopted and was raising like his own since it was his dope his parents overdosed on.

Kunta loved his new life in the palace with his adoptive father and brother. He was an A-student, so he got everything he could possibly want and need, thanks to King Uche spoiling him rotten. It was safe to say shit was all good at home - well, that was until Sanka manipulated a naive Kunta, and convinced him that King Uche was the enemy and needed to be executed immediately.

With the order given, the toy soldier went on his suicide mission. Sanka wasn't worried about him getting captured and squealing on him. His pops was dope game royalty and had a unit of head busters at his side at all times. Even if Kunta did manage to take the old man off his feet, he still had his bodyguards to contend with. These niggas were military trained and would blow the young homie off the map. Well, at least that was what Sanka was counting on. It was too bad that fate would show that he was completely wrong about Kunta.

Sanka nodded understandingly. Rubbing his chin, he took in the living room, looking for a way to escape. Unfortunately, the only way he was getting out of that mansion was if he was dead. Though it was a hard pill to swallow, he accepted it.

"Aaaaaaaah!" Sanka screamed like a madman, charging at his father and lifting the machete above his head. He knew he most likely wouldn't survive what was sure to come next but he figured it would make for one hell of a story to tell those sentenced to eternal damnation.

All of the African hitters turned their assault rifles on Sanka as he charged at his father at top-speed. They were about to cut his black ass down until King Uche lifted his hand. After the signal was given, the wig splitters lowered their weapons and looked on, wondering how things were going to play out.

King Uche pointed his Thompson at Sanka, closed his eyes, and rolled his head around his shoulders. He popped his eyes back open and tears slid down his meaty cheeks.

"Dear, Heavenly Father, please accept my boy into your glorious kingdom with open arms," King Uche said under his breath, drawing a bead on his only son with his submachine gun. Sanka made it halfway across the living room before he finally pulled the trigger. The Tommy gun rattled to life in his hands spitting a line of fire. Sanka stumbled back quickly and dropped his machete. He spun around in a 180-degree turn and slammed into the floor. He lay on his stomach, eyes bugged, mouth open, blood pouring from every wound in his body.

King Uche allowed the warm Thompson to cool in his lap. He ordered Abdullah and Hakim to snatch up Sanka's body and deliver it to a mortician he did a lot of business with. The men did like they were told and closed the doors behind them. King Uche yanked a handkerchief from its hiding place in his electric wheelchair. He dabbed the wetness from his eyes and wiped his snotty nose with it. He then cleared his throat and composed himself.

King Uche looked at Martin, whose eyes were pinned on Sanka's corpse. Though he wanted to be the one to bring his life to an end, he found satisfaction in seeing his demise.

May you rest in shit, Martin thought with a scowl. His top lip was curled in a sneer, making him look like an angry hound.

King Uche noticed the hate in his eyes as he watched his hands carry away Sanka's body. He also took note of his being the only white person present. Feeling eyes on him, Martin looked up and locked eyes with King Uche.

"Tell me, what grievance did my son cause you?" King Uche asked.

"That kid of yours was a piece of shit," Martin began. "He set off an explosive that killed five women, one of whom was my employer and close friend," he admitted. "I'd planned to exact my revenge but you obviously beat me to the punch, Pops."

King Uche nodded understandingly, but he didn't say anything. He knew his son was a rotten son of a bitch that deserved to die for all of the bad he had done. He had been the one to kill him, so as far as he was concerned, his debt had been paid with his life.

"Get these people back upon their feet and unshackled!" King Uche said to his hands.

One of them walked around with a shiny metal handcuff key. He unlocked the metal bracelets one by one. The hostages rose from the floor one after another rubbing their tender wrists. Toya and Martha ran into Ramone's arms. He hugged them as they kissed his cheeks. He found King Uche staring at him and wondered what was going through his mind.

"Young man, what is your name?" King Uche asked, stroking his beard.

Ramone had a feeling shit was about to get real active, so he pulled Martha and Toya behind him to act as a human shield for them. He searched the floor for anything he could defend himself, with but didn't come across anything.

"My name's Ramone...Ramone Seriki."

"Hmmm," King Uche narrowed his eyes and tilted his head. Ramone reminded him of someone familiar. "You wouldn't be any kin to Azubuike Seriki, would you?"

"Baby boy, that's your grandfather, your father's father," Martha whispered over his shoulder.

Right then, Ramone flashed back to the picture his pops gave him at Toya. "Yeah. That's my grandfather."

"Yeah. I can see it." King Uche smiled. "Your grandpa and I have a long history. Not only was he my chief enforcer, he was my brother, and the only man I ever trusted." Ramone nodded and wondered what the fuck he was telling him all of this for. "You come from good stock, son. Your grandpa, may he rest in paradise, made a fine soldier."

"Thanks," Ramone replied, hanging his arms around Martha and Toya's shoulders.

They walked towards the doors of the mansion with Jabari, Scorpion, Paperchase, and Martin fell in step behind them.

160

Chapter 25

Two African hitters stood in front of the doors holding assault rifles. When everyone approached them, they formed an X with their assault rifles, prohibiting them from leaving. Everyone frowned. Wondering what the fuck was up, they looked over their shoulder. King Uche maneuvered the small joystick on the arm of his electric wheelchair and spun around to those he'd freed from their bondages. He drove up to them.

"Yo, what the fuck is up?" Scorpion asked.

"That's what I wanna know." Jabari chimed in.

"What's up, OG?" Paperchase inquired.

"I still need a distro for New York. Do I have any takers?" King Uche asked, looking at the faces of all of the men standing before him. Everyone except Ramone confirmed they wanted to be the distro for New York. "What about you, son?"

Martha and Toya looked up at Ramone to see what his answer would be. He looked from his mother to his girl and then back up at King Uche. "I'm with it."

"Wait a minute, old man," Jabari interjected. "You only need one of us to hold down distribution out here. So which one of us is it gon' be?"

"The four of you will duel to the death," King Uche told him. "The winner will be the last man standing. My successor. And the sole distributor of Rebirth here."

Although Jabari, Paperchase, and Scorpion knew their lives were on the line it didn't change their minds. They were still with the shits. They agreed to participate in the duel. Now all they had to do was wait to see if Ramone was down with it.

"Baby, there's something I need to tell you before you make your decision," Toya told Ramone, taking his hand into both of hers. Now that she knew death was a possible outcome in this duel that was mentioned, she felt compelled to get something off her chest.

"What's that?" Ramone asked, rubbing her cheek.

Toya placed his hand on her stomach and smiled up at him. "I'm pregnant."

The biggest smile spread across Ramone's lips. He kissed her, lifted her up and spun around in circles. When he set her back down, they kissed a while longer.

"I'm gonna be a dad, yo. You hear that, Ma?" Ramone turned to his mother. She nodded as she wiped away tears of joy and embraced him.

"Babe, let's just get outta here," Toya told him, holding his hand again. "This duel is 'til death and I don't wanna risk losing you."

"She's right, baby boy." Martha chimed in. "We've already lost so much. We can't stand to lose you, too."

"I feel y'all, both of y'all." Ramone told them. "But with the baby coming now, and Momma needin' the bread to fight this virus, I gotta make something shake."

"Ramone, you forgot we're still sitting on my father's work and money," Toya reminded him. "Baby, we can flip that shit, invest it, and have enough change to take care of everybody."

"I hear you, boo, but that ain't gonna be enough," Ramone assured her. "We need a bag. We need a really big bag. And with the way this Rebirth shit hitting, we can run up a check like this." He snapped his finger.

Martha and Toya broke down crying like never before. They were terribly fearful of losing Ramone. They knew that once his mind was made up there wasn't any way they could change it, so they decided to support his decision. They gathered for a group hug. Ramone held the most important women in his life and kissed them both on top of their heads. A part of him wanted to cry with them but he had to be the pillar of strength in the situation.

You owe me a body. Jayshawn's voice played in Ramone's mind from that night he appeared to him in their apartment. He would use the vow he made to his brethren to fuel his motivation to win.

"What's it going to be, Ramone? Are you in or are you out?" King Uche inquired. Everyone who'd agreed to the duel was staring at him, awaiting his decision.

Ramone locked eyes with Jabari before giving his answer. He had a look in his eyes that told Jabari he was going to try his best to kill him. Jabari retorted with an evil smile, accepting the challenge the young shooter put on the table.

"I'm ten toes down," Ramone finally answered.

"Excellent." King Uche smirked.

"You know it's not too late to back out of this thing," Scorpion told Paperchase. He spared his brother's life once before because he couldn't bring himself to kill him. He hated for that deed to be in vain on the account of this duel.

Paperchase stared into his eyes for a moment before responding. "I know. And I will, right after you." Paperchase wasn't going to bow out gracefully if his brother was going to compete. He wanted to show him that he was his equal. That he was as fearless and as gangsta as he was.

"May the best gangsta win," Scorpion lifted his hand.

"May the best gangsta win," Paperchase slapped hands and embraced his brother. They patted each other on the back before breaking their hug.

***

Now that everyone had agreed to the duel, it was time to get shit cracking. Everyone cleared out of the mansion, leaving only those who were going to be participating in the game behind. Ramone's, Jabari's, Paperchase's, and Scorpion's hearts were racing and their adrenaline was pumping. The tension in the air was as thick as one of those big booty bitches at KOD and death was certain for everyone in the room except the victorious one.

Ramone, Jabari, Paperchase, and Scorpion stood in the four corners of the living room. They mugged each other and made death threats they promised to keep. They were interrupted when the doors opened again and four Black Barbie Dolls emerged. One of them pushed a cart with four lacquered black wood boxes on it. Engraved on them was a "U" with a jeweled crown on it, which stood for King Uche. The Black Barbie Dolls opened the boxes. In each box was a gold, eight-shot .22 magnum revolver and eight gold bullets wedged in a bed of velvet.

"Each of you will be given a Magnum revolver," King Uche's voice rang from the loud speakers. "You'll have a total of eight shots to try to eliminate one another. The last man standing will be victorious, my future successor, and a distro of the most potent heroin known to men—Rebirth."

While King Uche was talking, the Black Barbie Dolls blindfolded Ramone, Jabari, Paperchase, and Scorpion with black bandanas. They then placed a gold pistol into the hand that each man desired, kissed them on the cheek, told them "Good luck'", and rolled the cart out of the doors, locking it behind them.

"Gentlemen, you will now turn around in circles until I tell you to stop. Once I give the word, that's your cue to start firing, understood?" Ramone, Jabari, Paperchase, and Scorpion nodded almost simultaneously. "Good. Now turn in circles!" Everyone did as they were told until they were told to stop. They were left dizzy and off balance. This was exactly how King Uche wanted them. "Let the game begin!"

King Uche's voice rang out loud and thunderous. Right after, the hammers of the gold revolvers were being cocked back and shots were flying one after another. Bullets whizzed by Jabari and Paperchase. One nicked Scorpion's cheek. Another one pierced Ramone's shoulder. He howled in pain and clutched his wound.

"Gaaaah!" Jabari hollered as a bullet went through his thigh, dropping him to one knee. He upped his gun and started firing aimlessly since he couldn't see. Scorpion screamed in agony as heat seared his torso. He staggered backwards, holding his bleeding wounds.

"Fuck off my brotha, Blood!" Paperchase shouted, sending fire in the direction he believed the culprit was that blasted his brother. Although they were playing a Game of Death, he still felt obligated to protect his sibling.

Unfortunately, the bullets marred the walls, shattered vases and knocked portraits off the wall.

Slugs flew back and forth across the room. Ramone reacted to a slug like it was a mosquito when it flew dangerously close to his ear. A second one tore through the hip of his jeans. He dropped to the floor like he was about to do push-ups, listened closely, and fired at whomever he thought was the closest. He winded up missing his intended target, Paperchase, by an inch.

The bullets continued to fly back and forth. Ramone lay where he was, wincing from his shoulder wound and waiting for the perfect time to take his shot. Silence fell on the room. Everyone was breathing heavily and swallowing spit. One after another, they slowed their labored breaths and breathed through their noses. They had their guns outstretched before them as they moved around the room quietly, each keeping one hand on the wall. Their necks were on a swivel, listening intensely to everything around them.

A fly zipped around the room. It landed on Scorpion's nose and crawled inside of his left nostril. He sneezed and alerted everyone to where he was standing. One after another, Ramone, Jabari, and Paperchase pointed their gold pistols in his direction and lit his ass up. Bullet after bullet melted into Scorpion's chest and torso. He staggered forward, bleeding at the mouth. He dropped his pistol and fell face first to the floor. Blood poured out of his wounds like buckets of paint. He took three more breaths. The very last one brought his life to an end.

Boom, boom, boom, boom!

The trade of gunfire was loud as fuck inside of the living room. Then came the cries of agony, the grunts of the hurt, and the scream of excruciation. Ramone was the first to collide with the floor. He listened to Jabari and Paperchase exchange bullets while he blindly checked for where he'd been hit. He caught a hot one in his side and in his chest. He was in a lot of pain, but he knew the gunfight wasn't over until someone was triumphant.

Thud, thud!

One body dropped. A few seconds later another one dropped.

The sound of the two possibly falling to their death stole Ramone's attention from his wounds. He listened to see if there was anyone alive beside him as he bled out. The moment he heard a metallic click, he knew there was one participant left. He figured they had to be checking to see how many bullets they had left. With this action, Ramone knew exactly where they were in the living room. As quietly as he could, Ramone popped open the cylinder of his gold pistol and felt the eight holes that housed the bullets. He had one bullet left and he had to make it count.

Ramone tried to close the cylinder gently but it wound up making a low click sound. He cussed silently, knowing he'd given his location away. He and the man standing in his way of victory used the last of their strength to point their pistols where they believed each other was.

Then at the exact same time they cocked back their hammers and opened fire.

Chapter 26

Ramone stood in front of the full-length body mirror. His hands traveled over the old gunshot wounds he'd suffered in the gun battle back at the mansion. Growing up in the projects, he'd had many near death experiences but that night was by far the closest he'd come to losing his life. Ramone believed it was due to the grace of God and the spirit of his brother Jayshawn that he was victorious. It was the Lord who gave him the reassurance his aim was on point and it was Jayshawn who gave him a steady hand.

It was Jabari's bullet that punched a hole in Ramone's side and left him wearing a shit-bag for the rest of his life while it was Ramone's well-placed bullet that blew Jabari's brain out the back of his skull. There were some Nigerian paramedics under King Uche's thumb that stopped his bleeding and rushed him to the hospital. The blood transfusion was successful. Ramone would go on to make a full recovery and once he walked through the doors of Brookdale University Hospital, he'd be crowned the King of the Trenches.

Ramone strapped on a white Kevlar bulletproof vest, slipped his undershirt over his head, and put on his dress shirt. After fixing his platinum cufflinks, he looped his tie over his head and began tying it. A smile formed on his lips, seeing his pregnant wife enter their spacious bedroom through the mirror's reflection. Toya's face was beaten and her hair was laid to the gods. Her diamond earrings looked like small chandeliers and her diamond-studded necklace shimmered like the moon's reflection on the ocean at night. A black quarter length mink adorned her body and her form fitting black dress showed off her pregnant belly. It looked like she was hiding a basketball underneath her dress.

Ramone couldn't stop thinking of how beautiful Toya was to him. She'd always been beautiful, but now that she was pregnant with his prince, he found her more beautiful than she'd ever been.

"Here you go, baby." Toya grinned, presenting him with a glass of water and medication for his PTSD.

Ramone tossed back the medication and chased it with the glass of water. Toya adjusted his tie around the collar of his dress shirt and finished tying his tie. She kissed him and indulged in his glass of water.

"The fellas here?" Ramone asked Toya and disappeared inside the walk-in closet. He returned to the bedroom, sticking a nickel-plated .45 semi-automatic into the black leather holster in the small of his back.

"Yeah. They're down in the living room watching the fight," Toya replied, setting the empty glass on the dresser. When she turned around, Ramone was slipping into his jacket and buttoning it. Walking up to her, he wrapped his arms around her and stared into her eyes.

"Where's J.J.?" Ramone inquired about his first born, Jay-shawn Jr. He'd named him in honor of his older brother, God rest his soul.

"After your mother gave 'em a bath, he went right to sleep."

"And where's she?"

"Playin' hostess to the fellas." Toya threw her arms around his neck. She stared into his eyes lovingly and they kissed. Closing her eyes, she rested her head against his shoulder and hummed Luther Vandross's "If This World Was Mine". Ramone, whose eyes were also closed, held her waist and slowly danced with her.

"Aye, what are you love birds doing up there? It's time to go," one of the fellas called up to them from downstairs.

Ramone thrust his wrist out and glanced at his Franck Muller. It was 8:30. They were due to be at the restaurant in thirty minutes for King Uche's 67th birthday celebration.

"Shit. We're gonna be late," Ramone declared. Toya asked for the time and he told her.

"Lemme grab his gift, babe." Toya picked up a box wrapped in gold wrapping paper with a red and gold bow on it.

Ramone took the box from her. She grabbed her designer handbag. He interlocked his fingers with hers and led her out of the bedroom.

***

Martin stood before the 75-inch television set, mimicking the punches thrown by the boxer wreaking havoc on his opponent. Jibbs stood beside him, cheering the very same boxer on. He held a Corona in one hand while he punched at the air with the other. Sitting on the opposite of them were Sankeesy and Martin's date having a girl talk. Everyone was so engrossed in what they were doing they hadn't noticed Ramone and Toya coming down the steps.

Martha, who had just handed Jibbs a Corona, was popping the cap on another bottle of beer to give to Martin. Martin thanked her, kissed her cheek, and turned his attention back to the fight.

"Well, if it isn't my beautiful daughter-in-law and my handsome son." Martha smiled. Since she'd given up heroin. She'd packed on a few pounds and was gorgeous as can be. With the support of her friends and family, momma was giving the virus one hell of a fight. "Give Momma a spin so she can see how beautiful she looks." Smiling, Toya did as her mother-in-law requested. "The Lord knows he truly blessed my son with the vision you are, young lady."

"Thanks, Ma." Toya blushed, kissing her on the cheek and hugging her.

"And look at my baby boy in this fly-ass suit," Martha started on Ramone, who struck some *GQ* magazine poses for her. "Boyyyy, you're as sharp as Cooda Brown."

Toya and Ramone laughed hardily. "Ma, who in the hell is Cooda Brown?"

"My grandmother used to say that every time she saw a handsome man dressed to the nines," Martha told him. "Cooda was a young man who was always snazzily dressed back in Mississippi. Everyone in town took note of his snazzy suits and fancy dress shoes."

"You're somethin' else, old lady." Ramone kissed his mother on the cheek and hung his arm around her shoulders. He then addressed Martin and Jibbs. "If you boys don't mind, my lovely wife and I would like to take our leave now."

***

A white Rolls-Royce Phantom pulled into a parking lot at the back of a restaurant and parked. A black Mercedes-Benz Sprinter van loaded with shooters pulled in behind it and parked directly behind it. The doors of the Phantom popped open. Ramone, Toya, Jibbs, Martin, and their dates stepped out. Gifts in hand, the couples walked across the parking lot, talking and laughing. Ramone's face scrunched and he abruptly stopped walking. He looked around like he was trying to pinpoint something. Noticing he wasn't among them, Toya and the others looked back at him.

"Baby, what's the matter?" a concerned Toya asked.

Jibbs and Martin drew their guns and looked around for any threats. The doors of the Mercedes-Benz Sprinter van slid open and a dozen shooters hopped out with some very heavy artillery. They scanned the parking lot, prepared to lay down those that posed a threat to their employer's life.

"Yo, Ramone, what's goodie?" Jibbs asked in a hushed tone. He was wondering what the fuck was up.

Ramone didn't respond to anyone. He did a 360-degree turn, looking at everything and everyone surrounding him. The shooters who'd just hopped out of the Sprinter van moved in to form a wall of protection around him and his wife.

"Y'all don't hear that?" Ramone asked.

"Hear what, kid?" Martin inquired, looking around.

"Baby, what're you talking about?" Toya said, looking around and listening for whatever he'd heard.

Ramone remained quiet. He listened closely for what had a stronghold on his attention. What he was hearing was coming across clearly now, and it was across the parking lot. Ramone shoved the shooters out of his way and broke across the parking lot. His tie flapped over his shoulder as he ran as fast as he could towards the voice. The shooters, Jibbs, Martin, Sankeesy and everyone else chased after him.

170

"Ramone, where are you going?" Toya called after him, holding her pregnant belly.

"What's the matter, kid?" Martin asked.

Ramone wiped the sweat from his forehead as he chased after the voice he was hearing. He was exhausted, but it was imperative he found where the voice was coming from. The further he ran, the louder and clearer the voice became. It was like he was listening to a movie through a surround sound system. A light shone at the center of the parking lot. Ramone figured that was the source of the voice. Still in motion, he glanced over his shoulder with a smile and pointed up at the light.

"I think it's coming from there! Can y'all see it?" Ramone turned back around and kept on running towards the light.

Toya, Jibbs, Martin, and Sankeesy were reaching out to him and screaming for him not to go into the light. Their voices fell on deaf ears because the light had his undivided attention. Ramone took an awkward step and fell to the pavement. He scrambled back upon his feet and jogged into the shining light. Holding his hand above his eyebrows, he narrowed his eyes and stared up into the light. He could see the person who was talking. They were looking down upon him.

"Sorry, Dunn, but chu win some and you lose some," the man behind the voice said.

Ramone frowned realizing the man was literally talking to him. The light drew Ramone into it. Martin leaped to grab his ankle, but missed it. He collided with the ground, wincing. His date and Jibbs grabbed him by his arms and helped him up. Toya, who was crying, stood in the spotlight calling up to him. Her voice was growing smaller and smaller the further Ramone was drawn into the light. He was going so fast into the sky his suit and tie were ruffling. His dreadlocks were blowing in the wind and his cheeks were rippling.

***

Ramone was zapped back to reality. He lay in the middle of the living room floor of the mansion. His face was balled up from the lighting in the room and Jabari's bullet that had pierced the side of his neck. Blood slid out the corner of his mouth while he held his wounded neck. Tears burst out of his eyes. When his vision came back into focus from the intense lighting, he found Jabari standing over him. He had a gun in one hand and what he assumed was *his* blindfold in the other. Jabari tossed the blindfold aside and looked down at Ramone. He watched the blood seep from between his fingers and the light in his eyes slowly die.

"To—to only be sixteen-years-old, you—you got mad heart," Jabari told him as best as he could with a broken jaw. The bullet Ramone fired struck him there, tearing through flesh and breaking a hell of a lot of teeth. "I'm proud—I'm proud to say, in yo' short time with Woo, it was an honor to call you—you gang. Real shit." He saluted him with the Blood gang sign. Afterwards, he tossed his gold pistol to the side and looked around at all of the dead bodies. A wicked smile curled the corners of his lips as he realized he was The Last Man Standing and victorious.

Jabari looked up at the ceiling and threw his arms up. He walked around in circles shouting through clenched jaws. "I did it— I did it! I won. I'm the king! I'm the king of the—gak, cack, gag!" Jabari abruptly coughed up blood. He frowned when he touched his lips and his fingertips came away bloody. He took stock of his wounds, and he'd been seriously injured. His adrenaline had been pumping crazily during the duel and now that things had slowed down. He saw he was bleeding profusely, and felt like he was on the brink of death.

Jabari felt lightheaded. His eyelids felt heavy, his legs were wobbly, and felt like Jell-O underneath him. *Can't believe this shit! Just when a nigga was about to have the streets on lock, some bullshit happens! Fuck,* Jabari thought before dropped down to his knees with his arms dangling at his sides. He fell on the side of his face. His lips moved like a fish out of water and blood leaked out of his mouth. *It's all good. A nigga gon' find a plug in Hell and be the man down there.*

As soon as Jabari took his last breath, the doors of the mansion burst open and two African paramedics rushed inside. One was carrying medical equipment while they both were pushing a gurney. Toya and Martha rushed in behind them, hysterically calling out to Ramone.

Chapter 27

Toya and Martha hung over the shoulders of one of the paramedics weeping and begging God for Ramone's life.

"Ladies, please," the other paramedic said to Toya and Martha, holding his finger to his lips.

Toya and Martha cried silently while the paramedic tending to Ramone checked the pulse in his neck. He immediately applied direct pressure to the young shooter's wounds. Then used gauze to tape it down to stop his hemorrhaging. The paramedic looked over his shoulder at his partner.

"Awright. Dis wun's pulse is as slow as a snail, but he's still alive," the paramedic said of Ramone's current condition. "How about dee otha wun?"

"Oh God. Thank you God! That you, Father." Martha wiped away her tears and hugged Toya lovingly. She'd never been so happy in her entire life.

The other paramedic, holding two fingers to Jabari's neck, looked to his partner and shook his head no.

"Okay. Well, help me get dis wun loaded on dee gurney so he can get medical attention, fast."

The other paramedic, looking down at Jabari, stood up crossing himself with the Holy crucifix sign. He then helped load Ramone onto the gurney and strapped him in. They rushed out the doors of the mansion and down the steps with Toya and Martha on their heels. King Uche and his hitters stood near the ambulance. They watched the paramedics load Ramone into the back of the emergency vehicle. Toya and Martha were about to climb into the back of it but one of the paramedics stopped them.

"Ladies, I'm sorry but only wun of you can come wit' us," the paramedic told them, holding up his hands. "I'll let chu decide, but you must hurry."

The paramedic ran around the ambulance to hop in behind the wheel, leaving Toya and Martha to themselves.

"Martha, you go ahead, just keep me updated on his condition." Toya told her.

Martha looked back and forth between Toya and the ambulance. After making up her mind, she held Toya at arm's length and looked into her eyes. "Nah. You've proved time and time again how much you're down for Ramone. You've been there for him more than I have so you ride along with him."

"Momma, are you sure?" Toya asked.

"Yes." Martha hugged and kissed her like she was her daughter. She nudged her in the direction of the ambulance. "Now hurry up, and get outta here."

Toya stared at Martha a tad longer before hugging her again and hopping into the back of the ambulance. She slammed the door shut behind her and the ambulance whisked Ramone away.

Martha stared at the ambulance, holding her hands together in prayer. "Lord, please, watch over my boy. I can't stand to lose him like I lost his brother."

Martha was startled when she turned around and saw King Uche, his hitters, and Martin behind her. Their demeanors were threatening and she felt like they intended to smoke her.

Martha, refusing to show any fear in the face of death, hocked up mucus and spat on the ground. She poked out her chest and held her head high. "If you're gonna kill me, then go right ahead. HIV was gonna eventually take me out this bitch anyway," she informed King Uche. "I only ask that you grant me one wish, and that's that you see to it that I'm laid to rest beside both my boys."

"Nonsense. I wouldn't think of harming the mother of my successor," King Uche assured her. "I want 'em out there makin' as much money as he possibly can. Now how is the boy supposed to focus if he's worried about what's going on with his mother?"

Martha's brows furrowed wondering what he had in store for her. "How do you plan on helping me? I'm basically a dead woman walking, with this disease eating away at me."

"Martha," King Uche began. "Do you mind if I call you Martha?"

"Not at all."

"Martha, in my country we have remedies passed down from our ancestors and natural herbs grown from the richest soil on earth," he assured her. "With the right alkaline diet, cleansing, and detoxification, you could be back to picture perfect health in a few months."

"Wait a minute." Martha frowned with teary eyes. "You're not fucking with me, are you? 'Cause—'cause what you're giving me here is a second chance at life." She wiped away the tears that spilled down her cheeks.

"Martha, I've never been known for my sense of humor."

"Oooh." Martha charged at King Uche with her arms open. Instantly, his hitters drew down on her, stopping her in her tracks. A frightened look came over her face and she threw her hands up.

King Uche, knowing what she had in mind, lifted his hand. The hitters took this as a cue to fall back, so they lowered their assault rifles. King Uche nodded at Martha. She jumped in his arms, hugging and kissing him. He grinned and rubbed her back.

"What about this monkey that's been riding my back? This dope—this dope has sunk its talons into me and it won't let me go," Martha cried.

King Uche whipped out his handkerchief. He gave it to her and watched her dab her eyes. "Like I was saying, back home we have remedies for every health issue you can imagine. So do not worry, Martha, you're in good hands. I swear upon my life." He lifted his hand.

Three triple black Lincoln Navigators with Nigerian flags on either side of them pulled up in the driveway. The drivers, all of whom were African, hopped out of the huge SUV's and opened the back door for their passengers.

"Should the kid pull through this, I want you acting as his enforcer, Jibbs," King Uche told him. Jibbs was walking along on one side of him and Martin was walking along on the other. "Martin, you're well-seasoned in this game. He's gonna need your street knowledge and wisdom. I'd like you to step up and be the young man's consigliere."

"I'm down for whatever, long as this pretty young thang is beside me." Jibbs hung his arm around Sankeesy's neck and kissed her on the cheek. She grabbed hold of his hand and smiled happily.

A man hadn't made her this happy in a long time and she didn't want the feeling to ever end.

"It will be my pleasure, King," Martin replied, cleaning the blood off his face with a handkerchief.

King Uche had done his homework on Jibbs and Martin. Neither one of the men had dirt on their street resumés and were damn good at what they did. He figured it was best he brought them into his organization where he could put their talents to use. It was during the gunfight for the King of the Trenches that he decided to extend the offer he had in mind. Now that they'd accepted it, they were officially a part of the family.

"Excellent. You gentlemen will ride with me," King Uche told them. "Sankeesy, Martha, you'll ride along with my men in the other truck. Tonight, we'll board my private jet and leave for the Motherland."

Everyone got inside of the bulletproof truck, leaving Martha staring up at the stars. She narrowed her eyes into slits as the occasional gust of wind blew her hair into her face. "Jayshawn, I believe within my heart you can hear me. I need you to watch over your brother, baby, make sure he comes back to us." Her voice began to crack emotionally. "I need him. Toya needs him. His unborn child needs him."

"Hey, Martha, are you still coming?" Sankeesy called out to her from the back window of the armored vehicle.

Martha took the time to sniffle and wiped the wetness from her eyes. Mustering up a smile, she turned around to Sankeesy. "Yeah. I'm still coming, just gimme a second."

"Okay." Sankeesy replied before ducking back inside of the truck.

"Well, Momma's gotta get goin'. I'll talk to you later, sweetness." Martha blew a kiss up to the stars and made hurried footsteps to the truck. As soon as she slammed the door shut, the truck pulled off, followed by another and then another.

***

Once Ramone was loaded inside of the ambulance, the African paramedic took out his supplies to pack his wounds. After he was done, he removed a small gold treasure chest box with unique designs engraved into it. The African paramedic entered the combination code on the gold chest and it popped open. Inside there was a big gold syringe wedged inside of a purple velvet placement. Using his teeth, the African paramedic snatched the cap off the syringe and spat it aside.

Toya's face scrunched looking from the paramedic to the big gold syringe. She was curious as to what its contents were.

"What's that?" Toya asked. She stared at the gold syringe like it was a part that had fallen off an alien spacecraft.

"It contains the nectar from the fruits the Tree of Life bore," the African paramedic informed her as he rubbed a cotton swab saturated in alcohol on a vein on the inside of Ramone's arm.

"What's it supposed to do?" Toya questioned. She wasn't so sure she trusted him with injecting whatever it was into Ramone's body. For all she knew he could be trying to kill him. With all they've been through she didn't trust a fucking soul.

"It will rejuvenate 'em. He'll be back better than ever," the African paramedic assured her. He went to pierce Ramone's vein with the syringe and felt fire slice through his arm. He hollered, dropped the syringe, and clutched his wounded arm. He looked at his bloody hand and then up at Toya.

"What's really inside that fuckin' syringe, yo?" Toya asked threateningly, holding a barber razor at him. She'd hidden it inside of her pussy before she was abducted. She was uncomfortable walking around with that hunk of metal in her womb, but thought it was well worth it with what was happening now.

"I told you." The African paramedic winced while holding his wound. Blood soiled the sleeve of his shirt and slid down his arm.

"Bullshit! I swear to God, if you don't tell me, I'm gonna carve you up somethin' nasty," she swore. "Fuck with me if you want to. I'm not the one."

"You need to listen to me very carefully, Miss," the African paramedic said. "Your boyfriend doesn't have much time. If you want him to live to be a father and eventually your husband, I suggest you allow me to give him this shot. I'm not making any guarantees, but it's a great chance it will save his life."

Toya, still holding the barber's razor on him, stared into his eyes. He seemed sincere, but she was still reluctant to trust him. She flipped flopped her decision back and forth across her mind. She glanced at Ramone, and the possibility of losing him made her sick to her stomach. Tears treaded down her cheeks. Sniffling, she wiped the tears away with the sleeve of her hoodie. She then looked back at the African paramedic.

"Okay. You can go ahead and give 'em the shot." Toya told him. "But I swear on the lives of me, my man, and our unborn child, should this prove to be something fishy, I'm bringing this bitch from ear to ear." She showed him how she was going to slit his throat with the razor.

The African paramedic nodded understandingly before penetrating the vein in Ramone's arm with it. A bead of sweat slid down the side of his face as he slowly pushed down on the plunger. Although he had faith in the injection he was giving Ramone, there was always the fear of things going left.

The African paramedic took the needle out of Ramone's arm, taped a cotton ball down over the pierced vein, and deposited the used syringe inside of the red hazard box.

"What do we do now?" Toya inquired after the shot.

"We wait," he replied, wiping the sweat from the side of his face.

Taking hold of Ramone's hand, Toya bowed her head and said a prayer over him. She caressed his forehead and kissed him tenderly on his lips. Toya and the paramedic watched Ramone closely. They waited for any sign of him being alive but one had yet to come.

"Come on. Come on. Come on," the African paramedic said under his breath, tapping his fingers against his leg impatiently. He'd given the shot probably one hundred times and it never failed to work its magic.

It was so quiet inside of the ambulance that Toya and the paramedic could hear the noise of the traffic outside. An eternity seemed to pass and then…absolutely nothing happened. Realizing something should have occurred by now, the African paramedic frowned and glanced at his watch. He checked Ramone's wrist and neck for a pulse—nothing! Worry spread across Toya's face and teardrops fell from her eyes. She swiped them away and snorted back snot. She watched as the paramedic placed his ear against Ramone's chest to listen for his heartbeat. Lifting his head, he looked at Toya regretfully, shaking his head.

Toya bowed her head and sobbed out of control. The African paramedic, feeling terribly sorry for her loss, hugged her into him. He rubbed her back comfortingly and hushed her crying. Looking over his shoulder, his eyebrows wrinkled when something caught his eye.

Did he—did he just move his finga? the African paramedic thought, but wasn't exactly sure.

Feeling something was wrong, Toya looked up at him with a frown. "What's the matter?" she asked, following his line of vision which led her to Ramone.

"I thought I saw his finga move," the African paramedic replied. He went to check Ramone's vital signs again and he scared the living shit out of him. Ramone rose up in a flash, gasping for air like he was being held under water.

"Haaaaaaaaaaaaaaaaaaaaaaa!"

A wide-eyed Ramone, whose heart was beating like a tribal drum, looked around frantically. All of his senses seemed heightened. A tingling sensation surged up and down his body before disappearing at his fingertips and toes. Toya and the paramedic looked at him in astonishment. They watched as he looked at his hands like they didn't belong to him and then took stock of his gunshot wounds. There wasn't any trace of them being in the identified areas. It was as if his being shot had never happened.

Ramone locked eyes with Toya. She smiled through the tears sliding down her cheeks and threw her arms around his neck. Holding her in his arms, Ramone couldn't stop thinking of how blessed he was to be alive. The African paramedic smiled and gave him a thumb up. He grinned and returned the gesture.

The End

Lock Down Publications and Ca$h Presents assisted publishing packages.

BASIC PACKAGE $499
Editing
Cover Design
Formatting

UPGRADED PACKAGE $800
Typing
Editing
Cover Design
Formatting

ADVANCE PACKAGE $1,200
Typing
Editing
Cover Design
Formatting
Copyright registration
Proofreading
Upload book to Amazon

LDP SUPREME PACKAGE $1,500
Typing
Editing
Cover Design
Formatting
Copyright registration
Proofreading
Set up Amazon account
Upload book to Amazon
Advertise on LDP Amazon and Facebook page

***Other services available upon request. Additional charges may apply
Lock Down Publications
P.O. Box 944
Stockbridge, GA 30281-9998
Phone # 470 303-9761

Submission Guideline

Submit the first three chapters of your completed manuscript to ldpsubmissions@gmail.com, subject line: Your book's title. The manuscript must be in a .doc file and sent as an attachment. Document should be in Times New Roman, double spaced and in size 12 font. Also, provide your synopsis and full contact information. If sending multiple submissions, they must each be in a separate email.

Have a story but no way to send it electronically? You can still submit to LDP/Ca$h Presents. Send in the first three chapters, written or typed, of your completed manuscript to:

LDP: Submissions Dept
Po Box 944
Stockbridge, Ga 30281

DO NOT send original manuscript. Must be a duplicate.

Provide your synopsis and a cover letter containing your full contact information.

Thanks for considering LDP and Ca$h Presents.

<u>NEW RELEASES</u>

FOREVER GANGSTA 2 by ADRIAN DULAN

GORILLAZ IN THE TRENCHES by SAYNOMORE

JACK BOYS VS DOPE BOYS by ROMELL TUKES

MURDA WAS THE CASE by ELIJAH R. FREEMAN

KING OF THE TRENCHES 3 by GHOST & TRANAY
ADAMS

STRAIGHT BEAST MODE III
De'Kari
KINGPIN KILLAZ IV
STREET KINGS III
PAID IN BLOOD III
CARTEL KILLAZ IV
DOPE GODS III
Hood Rich
SINS OF A HUSTLA II
ASAD
RICH $AVAGE III
By Martell Troublesome Bolden
YAYO V
Bred In The Game 2
S. Allen
THE STREETS WILL TALK II
By Yolanda Moore
SON OF A DOPE FIEND III
HEAVEN GOT A GHETTO II
SKI MASK MONEY II
By Renta
LOYALTY AIN'T PROMISED III
By Keith Williams
I'M NOTHING WITHOUT HIS LOVE II
SINS OF A THUG II
TO THE THUG I LOVED BEFORE II
IN A HUSTLER I TRUST II
By Monet Dragun
QUIET MONEY IV
EXTENDED CLIP III

THUG LIFE IV

By **Trai'Quan**

THE STREETS MADE ME IV

By **Larry D. Wright**

IF YOU CROSS ME ONCE II

ANGEL IV

By **Anthony Fields**

THE STREETS WILL NEVER CLOSE IV

By **K'ajji**

HARD AND RUTHLESS III

KILLA KOUNTY III

By **Khufu**

MONEY GAME III

By **Smoove Dolla**

JACK BOYS VS DOPE BOYS III

A GANGSTA'S QUR'AN V

COKE GIRLZ II

COKE BOYS II

By **Romell Tukes**

MURDA WAS THE CASE III

Elijah R. Freeman

THE STREETS NEVER LET GO III

By **Robert Baptiste**

AN UNFORESEEN LOVE IV

By **Meesha**

MONEY MAFIA II

By **Jibril Williams**

QUEEN OF THE ZOO III

By **Black Migo**

VICIOUS LOYALTY III

By Kingpen

A GANGSTA'S PAIN III

By J-Blunt

CONFESSIONS OF A JACKBOY III

By Nicholas Lock

GRIMEY WAYS III

By Ray Vinci

KING KILLA II

By Vincent "Vitto" Holloway

BETRAYAL OF A THUG II

By Fre$h

THE MURDER QUEENS III

By Michael Gallon

THE BIRTH OF A GANGSTER III

By Delmont Player

TREAL LOVE II

By Le'Monica Jackson

FOR THE LOVE OF BLOOD II

By Jamel Mitchell

RAN OFF ON DA PLUG II

By Paper Boi Rari

HOOD CONSIGLIERE II

By Keese

PRETTY GIRLS DO NASTY THINGS II

By Nicole Goosby

PROTÉGÉ OF A LEGEND II

By Corey Robinson

IT'S JUST ME AND YOU II

By Ah'Million

BORN IN THE GRAVE II
By Self Made Tay
FOREVER GANGSTA III
By Adrian Dulan
GORILLAZ IN THE TRENCHES II
By SayNoMore

Available Now

RESTRAINING ORDER **I & II**
By **CA$H & Coffee**
LOVE KNOWS NO BOUNDARIES **I II & III**
By **Coffee**
RAISED AS A GOON I, II, III & IV
BRED BY THE SLUMS I, II, III
BLAST FOR ME I & II
ROTTEN TO THE CORE I II III
A BRONX TALE I, II, III
DUFFLE BAG CARTEL I II III IV V VI
HEARTLESS GOON I II III IV V
A SAVAGE DOPEBOY I II
DRUG LORDS I II III
CUTTHROAT MAFIA I II
KING OF THE TRENCHES

By **Ghost**
LAY IT DOWN **I & II**
LAST OF A DYING BREED I II
BLOOD STAINS OF A SHOTTA I & II III
By **Jamaica**
LOYAL TO THE GAME I II III
LIFE OF SIN I, II III
By **TJ & Jelissa**
BLOODY COMMAS I & II
SKI MASK CARTEL I II & III
KING OF NEW YORK I II,III IV V
RISE TO POWER I II III
COKE KINGS I II III IV V
BORN HEARTLESS I II III IV
KING OF THE TRAP I II
By **T.J. Edwards**
IF LOVING HIM IS WRONG…I & II
LOVE ME EVEN WHEN IT HURTS I II III
By **Jelissa**
WHEN THE STREETS CLAP BACK I & II III
THE HEART OF A SAVAGE I II III IV
MONEY MAFIA
LOYAL TO THE SOIL I II III
By **Jibril Williams**
A DISTINGUISHED THUG STOLE MY HEART I II & III
LOVE SHOULDN'T HURT I II III IV
RENEGADE BOYS I II III IV
PAID IN KARMA I II III
SAVAGE STORMS I II III
AN UNFORESEEN LOVE I II III

By **Meesha**

A GANGSTER'S CODE I &, II III

A GANGSTER'S SYN I II III

THE SAVAGE LIFE I II III

CHAINED TO THE STREETS I II III

BLOOD ON THE MONEY I II III

A GANGSTA'S PAIN I II

By J-Blunt

PUSH IT TO THE LIMIT

By **Bre' Hayes**

BLOOD OF A BOSS **I, II, III, IV, V**

SHADOWS OF THE GAME

TRAP BASTARD

By **Askari**

THE STREETS BLEED MURDER **I, II & III**

THE HEART OF A GANGSTA I II& III

By **Jerry Jackson**

CUM FOR ME I II III IV V VI VII VIII

An **LDP Erotica Collaboration**

BRIDE OF A HUSTLA **I II & II**

THE FETTI GIRLS **I, II& III**

CORRUPTED BY A GANGSTA I, II III, IV

BLINDED BY HIS LOVE

THE PRICE YOU PAY FOR LOVE I, II ,III

DOPE GIRL MAGIC I II III

By **Destiny Skai**

WHEN A GOOD GIRL GOES BAD

By **Adrienne**

THE COST OF LOYALTY I II III

By Kweli

A GANGSTER'S REVENGE **I II III & IV**

THE BOSS MAN'S DAUGHTERS I II III IV V

A SAVAGE LOVE **I & II**

BAE BELONGS TO ME I II

A HUSTLER'S DECEIT I, II, III

WHAT BAD BITCHES DO I, II, III

SOUL OF A MONSTER I II III

KILL ZONE

A DOPE BOY'S QUEEN I II III

TIL DEATH

By **Aryanna**

A KINGPIN'S AMBITON

A KINGPIN'S AMBITION **II**

I MURDER FOR THE DOUGH

By **Ambitious**

TRUE SAVAGE I II III IV V VI VII

DOPE BOY MAGIC I, II, III

MIDNIGHT CARTEL I II III

CITY OF KINGZ I II

NIGHTMARE ON SILENT AVE

THE PLUG OF LIL MEXICO II

CLASSIC CITY

By **Chris Green**

A DOPEBOY'S PRAYER

By **Eddie "Wolf" Lee**

THE KING CARTEL **I, II & III**

By **Frank Gresham**

THESE NIGGAS AIN'T LOYAL **I, II & III**

By **Nikki Tee**

GANGSTA SHYT **I II &III**

By **CATO**

THE ULTIMATE BETRAYAL

By **Phoenix**

BOSS'N UP **I , II & III**

By **Royal Nicole**

I LOVE YOU TO DEATH

By **Destiny J**

I RIDE FOR MY HITTA

I STILL RIDE FOR MY HITTA

By **Misty Holt**

LOVE & CHASIN' PAPER

By **Qay Crockett**

TO DIE IN VAIN

SINS OF A HUSTLA

By **ASAD**

BROOKLYN HUSTLAZ

By **Boogsy Morina**

BROOKLYN ON LOCK I & II

By **Sonovia**

GANGSTA CITY

By **Teddy Duke**

A DRUG KING AND HIS DIAMOND I & II III

A DOPEMAN'S RICHES

HER MAN, MINE'S TOO I, II

CASH MONEY HO'S

THE WIFEY I USED TO BE I II

PRETTY GIRLS DO NASTY THINGS

By Nicole Goosby

TRAPHOUSE KING **I II & III**

KINGPIN KILLAZ I II III

STREET KINGS I II

PAID IN BLOOD **I II**

CARTEL KILLAZ I II III

DOPE GODS I II

By **Hood Rich**

LIPSTICK KILLAH **I, II, III**

CRIME OF PASSION I II & III

FRIEND OR FOE I II III

By **Mimi**

STEADY MOBBN' **I, II, III**

THE STREETS STAINED MY SOUL I II III

By **Marcellus Allen**

WHO SHOT YA **I, II, III**

SON OF A DOPE FIEND I II

HEAVEN GOT A GHETTO

SKI MASK MONEY

Renta

GORILLAZ IN THE BAY **I II III IV**

TEARS OF A GANGSTA I II

3X KRAZY I II

STRAIGHT BEAST MODE I II

DE'KARI

TRIGGADALE I II III

MURDAROBER WAS THE CASE I II

Elijah R. Freeman

GOD BLESS THE TRAPPERS I, II, III

THESE SCANDALOUS STREETS I, II, III

FEAR MY GANGSTA I, II, III IV, V

THESE STREETS DON'T LOVE NOBODY I, II

BURY ME A G I, II, III, IV, V

A GANGSTA'S EMPIRE I, II, III, IV

THE DOPEMAN'S BODYGAURD I II

THE REALEST KILLAZ I II III

THE LAST OF THE OGS I II III

Tranay Adams

THE STREETS ARE CALLING

Duquie Wilson

MARRIED TO A BOSS I II III

By Destiny Skai & Chris Green

KINGZ OF THE GAME I II III IV V VI

Playa Ray

SLAUGHTER GANG I II III

RUTHLESS HEART I II III

By Willie Slaughter

FUK SHYT

By Blakk Diamond

DON'T F#CK WITH MY HEART I II

By Linnea

ADDICTED TO THE DRAMA I II III

IN THE ARM OF HIS BOSS II

By Jamila

YAYO I II III IV

A SHOOTER'S AMBITION I II

BRED IN THE GAME

By S. Allen

TRAP GOD I II III

RICH $AVAGE I II

MONEY IN THE GRAVE I II III

By Martell Troublesome Bolden

FOREVER GANGSTA I II

GLOCKS ON SATIN SHEETS I II
By Adrian Dulan
TOE TAGZ I II III IV
LEVELS TO THIS SHYT I II
IT'S JUST ME AND YOU
By Ah'Million
KINGPIN DREAMS I II III
RAN OFF ON DA PLUG
By Paper Boi Rari
CONFESSIONS OF A GANGSTA I II III IV
CONFESSIONS OF A JACKBOY I II
By Nicholas Lock
I'M NOTHING WITHOUT HIS LOVE
SINS OF A THUG
TO THE THUG I LOVED BEFORE
A GANGSTA SAVED XMAS
IN A HUSTLER I TRUST
By Monet Dragun
CAUGHT UP IN THE LIFE I II III
THE STREETS NEVER LET GO I II
By Robert Baptiste
NEW TO THE GAME I II III
MONEY, MURDER & MEMORIES I II III
By **Malik D. Rice**
LIFE OF A SAVAGE I II III
A GANGSTA'S QUR'AN I II III IV
MURDA SEASON I II III
GANGLAND CARTEL I II III
CHI'RAQ GANGSTAS I II III
KILLERS ON ELM STREET I II III

JACK BOYZ N DA BRONX I II III
A DOPEBOY'S DREAM I II III
JACK BOYS VS DOPE BOYS I II
COKE GIRLZ
COKE BOYS
By Romell Tukes
LOYALTY AIN'T PROMISED I II
By Keith Williams
QUIET MONEY I II III
THUG LIFE I II III
EXTENDED CLIP I II
A GANGSTA'S PARADISE
By **Trai'Quan**
THE STREETS MADE ME I II III
By **Larry D. Wright**
THE ULTIMATE SACRIFICE I, II, III, IV, V, VI
KHADIFI
IF YOU CROSS ME ONCE
ANGEL I II III
IN THE BLINK OF AN EYE
By **Anthony Fields**
THE LIFE OF A HOOD STAR
By Ca$h & Rashia Wilson
THE STREETS WILL NEVER CLOSE I II III
By K'ajji
CREAM I II III
THE STREETS WILL TALK
By Yolanda Moore
NIGHTMARES OF A HUSTLA I II III
By King Dream

CONCRETE KILLA I II III
VICIOUS LOYALTY I II
By Kingpen
HARD AND RUTHLESS I II
MOB TOWN 251
THE BILLIONAIRE BENTLEYS I II III
By Von Diesel
GHOST MOB
Stilloan Robinson
MOB TIES I II III IV V VI
SOUL OF A HUSTLER, HEART OF A KILLER
GORILLAZ IN THE TRENCHES
By SayNoMore
BODYMORE MURDERLAND I II III
THE BIRTH OF A GANGSTER I II
By Delmont Player
FOR THE LOVE OF A BOSS
By C. D. Blue
MOBBED UP I II III IV
THE BRICK MAN I II III IV
THE COCAINE PRINCESS I II III IV V
By King Rio
KILLA KOUNTY I II III
By Khufu
MONEY GAME I II
By Smoove Dolla
A GANGSTA'S KARMA I II
By FLAME
KING OF THE TRENCHES I II III
by **GHOST & TRANAY ADAMS**

QUEEN OF THE ZOO I II

By **Black Migo**

GRIMEY WAYS I II

By Ray Vinci

XMAS WITH AN ATL SHOOTER

By Ca$h & Destiny Skai

KING KILLA

By Vincent "Vitto" Holloway

BETRAYAL OF A THUG

By Fre$h

THE MURDER QUEENS I II

By Michael Gallon

TREAL LOVE

By Le'Monica Jackson

FOR THE LOVE OF BLOOD

By Jamel Mitchell

HOOD CONSIGLIERE

By Keese

PROTÉGÉ OF A LEGEND

By Corey Robinson

BORN IN THE GRAVE

By Self Made Tay

MOAN IN MY MOUTH

By XTASY

BOOKS BY LDP'S CEO, CA$H

TRUST IN NO MAN

TRUST IN NO MAN 2

TRUST IN NO MAN 3

BONDED BY BLOOD

SHORTY GOT A THUG

THUGS CRY

THUGS CRY 2

THUGS CRY 3

TRUST NO BITCH

TRUST NO BITCH 2

TRUST NO BITCH 3

TIL MY CASKET DROPS

RESTRAINING ORDER

RESTRAINING ORDER 2

IN LOVE WITH A CONVICT

LIFE OF A HOOD STAR

XMAS WITH AN ATL SHOOTER

King of the Trenches 3

CPSIA information can be obtained
at www.ICGtesting.com
Printed in the USA
LVHW010734091222
734813LV00009B/555

9 781958 111505